Singing a Man to Death

short stories by

MATTHEW
FRANCIS

CinnamonPress

INDEPENDENT INNOVATIVE INTERNATIONAL

Published by Cinnamon Press,
Meirion House,
Tanygrisiau,
Blaenau Ffestiniog,
Gwynedd
LL41 3SU
www.cinnamonpress.com

British Library Cataloguing in Publication Data. A CIP record for this book can be obtained from the British Library.

Designed and typeset in Garamond by Cinnamon Press.
Cover design by Tanwen Haff
Cinnamon Press is represented by Inpress and by the Welsh Books Council in Wales.
Printed in Poland
The publisher acknowledges the support of the Welsh Books council

Acknowledgement is due to the following publications, in which some of these stories first appeared: *City Writings, Encounter, First Fictions: Introduction 10, Hyphen, Sing Sorrow Sorrow, The Third Alternative, New Welsh Review.*

Contents

Singing a Man to Death

Singing a Man to Death

I keep hearing the tune. Not out loud, of course. It's just that some mornings, usually when I've had too much to drink the night before, I wake up at first light and find it running through my head: *Mete üöbik oo tänabu.* It's been more than twenty-five years. And I only heard it once, or twice at the most. In any case nobody died of it, as far as I know. The music probably isn't fatal, no more than any other of those things that stay with you: the smell of toast, say, or the mauve fluttering the gas fire used to make when you lit it, or the scrape of a stylus across the shiny black grooves of a vinyl record. Remember how the silence before the track started used to be amplified, too? You could probably kill someone using memories if you kept at it long enough.

I used to keep all the essentials of life on a rug in front of the fire: a jar of coffee, a jar of Coffee-Mate, an electric kettle, bread, butter, honey, a toasting-fork improvised out of a wire coathanger, books and papers, a scattered trail of LPs that led to the stereo. The records mostly belonged to Luke, who had thrown out my *Simon and Garfunkel's Greatest Hits* and my *Crime of the Century* and my *Tubular Bells*, and was taking charge of my musical education. After an evening in the pub, we would end up in my room, which was bigger than Tobias's on the other side of the passage and more conveniently situated than Luke's attic-room. I would sit by the gasfire and make coffee while Luke hung over the stereo, so he could take off a record halfway through a track when he decided he'd grown out of it, and Tobias, as usual after a few pints, thrashed about heavily on the bed, claiming to be possessed.

'What is this place? How do I come here?'

'Who are you, man?' Luke would ask.

'I am not man. My name is Eliza Wilmot. I was born in the year of our Lord 1746. I am eighteen years old.'

'Yeah? Who's the king?'

'I know naught of kings and princes. I am a simple woman.'

'You are a simple arsehole.'

'Abuse me not, reprobate. I bring news of the life beyond, and of this life.'

'You're full of shit.'

'Not so. I have left this corporeal world and all its feculent matter. Now listen. Listen.'

'If you're a woman, how come you don't sound like one?'

'Listen to me, fools. The spirit is within thee. Harken to its voice. Its word is "Do what thou wilt." Do what thou wilt shall be the whole of the law. I have spoken.'

Then there would be a long pause, while he seemed to have fallen asleep, until I brought the mug of coffee close to his face. 'What? What? Where am I? What happened?'

Mete üöbik. Remember landladies? How they didn't like you flushing the toilet at night, or using Blutak on the walls, how the worst fear they had in the world was that you would go to bed with someone in their house? Jessie never knocked; she would just appear out of the shadows into the light of the anglepoise, wrinkled and froglike with a helmet of dyed black hair, a cryptic smile on her face. The three of us were in the same room; that constituted a party, and parties would wear out the house, just as surely as posters wore out the wallpaper and sex, if any of us ever managed to get any, would take all the bounce out of the bedsprings.

Jessie didn't shout. The worst she would ever say was 'You are not a worker,' in her peculiar voice, which sounded foreign even though its accent was pre-war upper-class English. 'At least Philip is a worker. Even Tobias is a worker. But Luke is *not* a worker!' She would throw her arms round Luke or me, smiling all the time in that unreadable way.

'Ah, good evening, my good woman!' Tobias would shout from the bed.

But she never seemed to hear him. 'Is he tired? He shouldn't be lying on the bed with his shoes on.'

'I expect she's from the Carpathians,' Tobias said one evening after Jessie had left. 'A lot of landladies are.'

'You are so full of shit,' Luke told him. 'You know that?'

Tobias twiddled the ends of his beard. 'There was a Carpathian landlady in Mill Road,' he said, 'who sang one of her tenants to death. Caught him in bed with someone and after that she would stand outside his door every night and sing to him. As they do in the Carpathians.'

Apparently there was a musical phrase called the Devil's Interval, which was considered unlucky in all musical traditions. But in the Carpathians, the Devil's Interval was just one element of an ancient murdersong, somehow kept back from the notebooks and tape-recorders of the folklorists. It could never be written down properly in any case, with its quartertones and nasal trills and the occasional noise generated deep inside the skull by an organ that most people don't possess in working order. It was passed on by the village bard-shaman-healer who would whisper-sing it on his deathbed to the chosen apprentice. Or *her* deathbed? Tobias wasn't sure.

'You'd have to have a good memory, in any case. You can only hear the song so many times before you die. It's one of the Numbers of Power. Seventy-seven, I believe. Or seven hundred and seventy-seven.'

'Seven hundred and seventy-seven what?'

'Reprises. Singings.'

'So let me get this straight—you just sing to someone and it kills them?'

'With your fingers in your ears, obviously,' Tobias said. 'Otherwise you would drop dead yourself.'

'That is so cool,' Luke said.

Luke used to break into my room through the window in the early morning and put a record on the stereo at full volume. 'How about this?' he would ask as I sprang up waving my arms.

'What? Oh God. Fuck off.'

'No, man, I'm serious. What do you think?'

'Turn it down.'

'All right, all right, cool. I made you a cup of coffee. Now what do you think?'

'Oh God. Yes, I quite like it. Yes, it's OK, great. What is it?'

'You have no fucking taste at all, have you?'

He was right. I had no natural taste in his kind of music, and had to work it all out for myself. It had nothing to do with being contemporary. The word he always used about a record he liked was 'authentic', and I gradually came to realise it meant dead. His heroes were Jimi Hendrix and Jim Morrison, Janis Joplin and Nick Drake, all suicides or as good as, all dead before they were thirty. I got to be able to recognise the suicide singers. There was a graveyard hollowness in the voice, as if the singer was already dead when recording it. The effect was even creepier on my record-player, which used to pick up radio messages from the local taxi-drivers and occasionally let off a deafening rat-tat-tat like a machine-gun firing out of the speakers. Luke would grab the record off the turntable and ask me when I last had my fucking stylus checked.

'It isn't the stylus,' I told him. 'It's just the speakers. It doesn't damage the record.'

'Haven't even got an anti-static cloth,' he mumbled.

'I use that sock. It's quite clean.'

'I'm fucking wasted on you, you realise that?'

Luke saw himself as a rock star *manqué*. He had the looks for it, supposedly, though I couldn't see it myself. His shoulders were so broad he looked slightly deformed, or as if there was a coathanger stuck in the back of his shirt, and his head, with its flouncy greying curls, was also exaggeratedly large. But he would study himself in the hall mirror on his way out to the front door for minutes at a time and sometimes, in the middle of a conversation, he would say, *à propos* of nothing, 'I'm Luke?' like that, with a question mark on the end of it, as if he couldn't believe how lucky he was. And this girl I knew, Yasmin, who had a boyfriend in Kettering, used to refer to him as 'your gorgeous friend', purely theoretically, in the same way she would talk about other women's eyes or figures.

I went up to his room one afternoon and found him lying on his floor, surrounded by naked LPs and tattered sleeves bearing black and white pictures of snowy pine forests, fat women in flouncy dresses and small men clutching zithers. 'How do you feel, man?' he shouted. 'Does this one make you feel kind of anaemic?'

'It's terrible.'

'That is the whole fucking point.'

'Put it off. I can't hear myself think.'

'Isn't it great?' Luke got up slowly, and put the record off. 'You want coffee?' he said as usual, but when I accepted he just stood there, shaking his head slightly, as if testing it for something. 'What do you want to hear yourself think for?' he said finally. 'Aren't you so fucking fed up with hearing yourself think?'

I knew what he meant, then. At least I was fed up with hearing myself think about Yasmin and the boyfriend she stayed with in Kettering most weekends. She showed me his picture once: solid-looking with a Beatle haircut and the points of his collar sticking out of a blue Marks and Spencer's sweater with a silver diamond-pattern on the front. They'd been going out for five years and were practically married. I found it hard to imagine life in Kettering, where people started going out at the age of fourteen. And I found it hard to imagine Yasmin, whose skin was golden even in the winter and whose eyebrows looked like Chinese calligraphy, in Kettering at all. I asked Luke once if he knew where it was and he said it was so unthere it didn't even exist.

I used to wake up at night and hear myself telling her how I'd always loved her, how I had so much more to offer than David because I was an intellectual and intellectuals made the best lovers. Then telling her that I was an intellectual and intellectuals could only make themselves and other people miserable, so she must go back to Kettering where she really belonged. Telling her that I knew we were only friends, but why shouldn't friends have sex? She was lonely away from David, I was lonely away from, well, nobody much, and there was such a lot we could teach each other before going back to our respective lives. And then, sooner or later, telling her that even though she didn't love me and I didn't love her, I needed her to please, please, sleep with me just this once and I would never bother her again.

At this point I used to get out of bed. The time was always somewhere between three and four-thirty, the brief period after the last drunk and before the milk float. The thoughts stopped at once, to be replaced by a raw, chafing feeling. Then I would sit in my knobbly blue armchair beside the gas fire and listen to records through the headphones. The ones Luke had lent me or made me buy, death music: Nick Drake and Janis Joplin, Jimi Hendrix and The Doors. The only ones that worked in the small hours of the morning beside the gas fire.

But this stuff? You couldn't even understand the words.

He rubbed his face with his fingers as if trying to remove a blush. 'All right,' he admitted.

'All right what?'

'It is crap, most of it. Well, all of it. I just wanted to find the right song. *The* song.'

He had somehow got it into his head that if the murdersong existed you must be able to buy it somewhere; in the record stall at the market or one of those backstreet shops that sold bootleg albums in plain sleeves. All his life he'd been looking for a kind of music that nobody else knew about, a musical Holy Grail, except that it had to be a dark one, a death grail. Now he had almost found it.

'You really believe it, don't you?' I said.

'Yeah. No. Well, look, I don't want to kill myself, if that's what you think. Not now, anyway—I'm not even twenty yet, for fuck's sake. Give it a few years, and maybe. Don't you get it?'

'No.'

'Aren't you even a bit curious? About what it would sound like, a song that was so powerful it could end your life? I mean, listen, man—' Luke started to pick up the albums and put them back in their sleeves. 'Would it hurt? Or would it be more like a drug, so that every time you listened to it you got higher and higher, until the last time, seventy-seventh or whatever, you just floated away into the other world? Or maybe it would be very subtle, so you didn't even know it was doing anything. It would be like you play it seventy-six times, and nothing happens. And then you put the record away and you'll always know that whatever happens to you in life, if you get cancer, or if some fucking bastard in the White House decides it's time for the Third World War, you can just get out your record and that's it.'

'If it works,' I said, but he wasn't listening.

'Or get this, right? You go through the rest of your life knowing that one day you might hear that song. Like you have kids, and one of them thinks, oh I'll just put that funny old record on, and you walk in at that moment and say oh God, not that one! But it's too late. Amazing, eh?'

'Yes, and the kid doesn't know that it was the record that made you drop dead, so he plays it another seventy-six times and dies himself.'

13

'Now you're getting it.'

'But that's crazy. Why should you want to kill your own child?'

'I don't, man, I don't even have a fucking child. This is a hypothetical child, right? If he can get himself born, he can look after himself from then on. OK, maybe I throw away the record for the sake of the kid. I still know that one day I might walk into a party and find they're playing my tune.'

'They wouldn't. It's crap.'

'So what? I'll be middle-aged by then. I'll be a chartered accountant, living in a semi-detached, mowing the lawn on Saturdays. I'll be going to parties where everybody wears ties and the music is just automatically crap. Except that in my case the crap would be like heroin, or Russian roulette or something, it would have an edge to it.'

'Look,' I said. 'First of all, you don't even know this song exists. It's just some stupid legend. Second, even if it's true, who on earth would make a record of a thing like that? It would be illegal, if it existed, which it doesn't. And thirdly, even if it exists, and it is on record, how the fuck are you going to know when you hear it? You said yourself there might not be any symptoms.'

'That's what I like about you,' Luke said. 'You're a wanker, but you're a really logical wanker.'

One day he broke into my room while I was out, made himself a cup of coffee and went away again, leaving a dozen of his Eastern European bargain albums behind. The note said, 'You're right, except maybe for one of these which has been giving me strange thoughts. I don't want to hear any of them ever again! Your turn now. Which is the mindfuck one?'

They reminded me of the ancient records we used to have in my childhood, piled up in a compartment of a pseudo-mahogany cabinet called the radiogram. Mono, all of them. I slipped one of them out—actually it fell out, having no inner sleeve, and wheeled across the carpet. The picture on the cover showed a large grey city, all pillars and pediments; the album appeared to be by somebody called Walmar Udmurt.

To my surprise, it had no scratches, just a couple of dull areas that might be a bit fuzzy or might play perfectly well. I carried it over to the stereo. Maybe I'd play a track, if only to prove that it couldn't do anything to me.

It was a marching band with city noises in the background, even a bit of birdsong, I thought, but no singing yet. The track had only been on a minute when the machine-gun went off through the speakers and, in my slightly nervous state, I thought my head would explode. I took the needle off and put the record back.

I didn't recognise at first what was wrong with Yasmin's face. Then I realised she had been crying and it had made her blurry, as if I was viewing her out of focus. This was one of the fantasies that kept me awake at night: Yasmin in tears, asking for an arm round her shoulders, a hug. I almost reached for her shoulders there and then, on the threshold, but thought better of it.

'What's the matter?' It was Sunday evening—she shouldn't even be here. Something must have happened in Kettering to make her come back early.

'It's nothing. David and I had a bit of a barney, that's all.'

I got the impression she'd been practising the phrase, trying to make it sound emotionally neutral, insignificant, even a bit of a joke. What would Luke have made of the word she used? *Barney*, what the fuck? That is such a non-word, man. I instinctively looked along the passage to the stairs before ushering her inside. No sign of him.

She didn't want coffee, she said. She'd been drinking tea for three hours already. So I offered her whisky, a bottle I'd had for my birthday and hardly touched.

'I don't like it.'

'Nor do I, much, but it'll make you feel better.'

'All right.'

We sat together on the rug in front of the gasfire, drinking whisky, while she cried. I'd never been this close to her before, not for so long, anyway. She was wearing a fluffy black cardigan that made her look like a kitten, and I kept thinking how strange it was to cover all that smoothness with something so hairy, those thin shoulders with all that padding. I could smell her tears.

'I always thought I was going to marry him, you see. Ever since I met him. And then suddenly, all at once, I'm on my own again. Do you know what it's like to be on your own?'

I felt wiser than I'd ever been in my life, as if I had lived everything that human beings were capable of. 'Everybody goes through that,' I said. 'But you're not alone. I'm here.'

'You're really sweet, Philip. Thank you.'

After a couple of whiskies, her mood started to change. She dried her tears and became recklessly cheerful. 'Sod him,' she kept saying, 'sod him, sod him. There are plenty more fish in the sea. And I've always got you, haven't I, Philip?'

'Of course you have.'

'Do you feel like dancing? I want to dance.' She kicked off her shoes and stood unsteadily on her black-stockinged feet in front of my gas fire. 'What music have you got?'

The trouble was, I didn't have anything suitable. She went through my record collection with an expression of growing impatience. 'They're not mine,' I said. 'Most of them belong to Luke.'

'Haven't you got anything like, oh, Doctor Hook? And what are all these foreign things?'

'They're Luke's.'

'Luke must be really weird. Don't you have any music of your own?'

'Luke threw it all out.'

'Oh, look at her. Isn't she beautiful?'

It was one of the East European records, with a picture of a woman on the cover. *Mete Üöbik*, it said, and underneath, Ježamin Rääkima. Presumably the name of the singer— rather like Yasmin, which seemed an omen. And yes, she was quite good-looking in a black-and-white, pearls-and-hairspray sort of way. I'd noticed her before when flicking though the records, but that was all.

'What's this one like, Philip?'

'Oh, it's… you wouldn't like it.'

'Let's try it. Come on, we could dance.'

'It's very old-fashioned. I don't think you could dance to it.'

'Oh go on. We could smooch anyway, you can smooch to anything. Don't you want to smooch with me, Philip?'

She was full of these words this evening. I looked at her standing by the record-player in her black fuzz and wanted desperately to smooch with her. My mind was working fast now, as if it had known all my life what to do in this situation. From the smooch in front of the gasfire to the gentle capsize on to the bed by the wall was only three and a half paces and I knew exactly how I was going to get there.

When you put on a record, assuming you do it right and don't jab your stylus down in the middle of a track, there is first no sound at all and then the sound of amplified silence. That can last as long as thirty seconds, rather pleasurable ones usually, in which you prepare yourself to listen. You find out also at this stage whether the recording is old and likely to be scratchy or not. This time it was not too bad, just a bit wheezy. But the silence seemed to last longer than usual, long enough to let me get back to the rug, hastily push the coffee things out of the way and wrap my arms round Yasmin's furry exterior, which collapsed in on itself as if I'd knocked all the air out of her. She was very small now. I'd got right inside, to the kernel of her. I could feel her body, naked under all those clothes, squeezing me back. Then the music started.

For hours after all this was over, I still thought that sound was bells, huge church bells of a kind I'd never heard. White-sounding was the phrase I used to myself, picturing bells made of some milk-coloured metal. They were playing a tune, but it was so overpowering that it seemed to be in my bones rather just than my ears. Then, over the top of it came an unnaturally deep voice, a flat guttural bass like someone vomiting in slow motion. The strange thing was that I somehow recognised the voice as belonging to that elegant woman on the album sleeve. It was a ghost voice, a voice that had ceased to be human.

Yasmin froze in my arms. 'Take it off.'

I ran to the record player and lifted up the needle. 'It's all right,' I told her when I'd got my breath back. 'It was on at the wrong speed, that's all. This record is a 78.'

'It was horrible.'

'Don't worry, it isn't meant to sound like that. It's just that my stereo doesn't play 78s. I'll put something else on for you.'

'No,' she said. 'That's all right. I'd better be going anyway.'

At about five in the morning, the first traffic noises started outside my window and I gave up trying to sleep. I got out of bed and crouched over the fire for a while. Then it occurred to me that the record that had ruined everything was still on the turntable. I took it off and put it back in its sleeve. That was when I realised what those milk-white church bells had been—of course, a piano. Probably at a normal speed it was a sweet little song about shepherdesses and babbling brooks. Good enough for smooching to, assuming Yasmin was right and you could smooch to anything. But she wasn't right, was she? There were some things you couldn't smooch to.

I gathered all the records together. They were mine, now, and I could do what I liked with them. Luke had probably never paid more than 50p each for them, in any case. If I'd had a real fire I would have thrown them on it and watched them burn or melt, probably both at once. As it was, I had an idea. I took the pearls-and-hairspray record out again, inserted the hook of my home-made toasting-fork through the hole in the middle, and sat down in front of the fire.

Mete üöbik oo tänabu. Me öitselind on tänavu. How delicate they were, records. You had to hold them by the edges, keep them out of the sun. Just breathing in their vicinity seemed risky. They played not only music, but every knock and scrape and slip and shake that had happened to them since they left the studio. Jessie probably looked on her house as a sort of record, one that endlessly replayed to her all the mess and clumsiness that was lived in it. Even the smell of toast, she claimed, could keep her awake at night. I wondered if the smell of scorched vinyl would disturb her. It was getting pretty smoky in the room by now, so I thought I'd better stop. In any case, the half-melted records weren't exactly disposed of. I put my clothes on and went for a walk. There were still very few people about and I was able to throw them in the river without being seen. To my relief, they sank.

And since nobody died as far as I know, I probably didn't hear the song again, that morning months later, just before we left for the summer. We were all going to be back in College next year, which didn't bother me much. Luke and I hadn't got on so well since I melted his records, which he claimed he'd only lent me and wanted back. Then there was the thing between him and Yasmin after Christmas, but at least that didn't last after the calamitous evening when Jessie walked in on them in bed. We ended up being polite to each other, Jessie and Luke, Luke and me, Yasmin and me, Luke and Yasmin probably. I had the feeling that maybe she had really got to him, the way she got to me. Except that he had the memories out of it, I suppose. All I kept were the fantasies, memories of fantasies.

So, tricked awake by the early dawn, I probably never did hear a voice floating down from the top of the house, a very high soprano, rather beautiful in a cracked sort of way:

> *Mete üöbik oo tänabu maeal läin*
> *Meie üöbik on tänävu muuale mend.*
> *Kord oli ühel vanal ausal mehel*
> *Me õitselind on tänavu maale läind.*

But I still remember it, somehow or other. And every time I think of it I have this vision of Jessie, her helmet of dyed black hair, her froglike face, standing on the dim stairs with a finger jammed into each ear, singing and singing.

American Fugue

My name is not Samuel Taylor Coleridge. It is also not Silas Tomken Cumberbatch, a name having the same initials. As a matter of fact, unlike most Americans, I don't have three names, only two, but people with three names always sound like murderers to me. How about Lee Harvey Oswald? Or Mark David Chapman? Or John Wilkes Booth, come to that? Sirhan Sirhan is a curious exception, a man who had only one name and doubled it. No doubt a psychiatrist could explain what connection if any this had with his crime. As for me, for a while back there I didn't have much idea who I was at all, but after all the identity crisis is part of the American Way of Life, and I am now happily married to my third wife, Elsa Hopkins Connolly, and living with my second, Eva Kohlrabi, who also has a third spouse somewhere. Eva is a charming woman with too much blonde hair and a bony little face like that of a cat. Perhaps the feline element explains her affinity for poets. At any rate it must have taken a lot of guts to come winding over the desert in her blue Volkswagen and confront Dean Overbird the way she did. The Dean had of course been aware for some time that I was living on campus with the Veggies (officially Associated Dietary Interest Group), one of the many factions into which the students of Desert Greens University are divided for social and residential purposes. Nevertheless, he didn't have much idea who I was either, as I had arrived in a simple blue suit with nothing in the pockets, and was pretty confused about everything except my art. So Eva took it upon herself to sort him out.

'He is a very distinguished man,' she told him, 'and he is ill. He won the National Book Award and the Pulitzer Prize for his volume *American Rubai'yat*, and has twice been the recipient of Guggenheim Fellowships. At present he is living in Los Angeles with his third wife and their daughter. Except that at present he is nowhere to be found and I have reason to believe that he is here.'

It was not clear how she traced me. In fact she had run into the Antelope Family, a Native American Country and Western group whom I had met somewhere in the desert. I was in such a vague state of mind that the experience of wandering among broken rocks and elaborate cactus trees didn't seem at all out of place and I remember Ron Antelope standing beside his battered minibus waving a joint and telling me that he'd lived in the desert all his life and couldn't get used to the fact that he wasn't somewhere else. He thought it was the influence of television, which is always showing programmes about tough cops from New York or Los Angeles. To me, on the other hand, Ron, his pretty wife who sang harmony, the baby, the blankets, the rhythm section and the vehicle they travelled in were as familiar at that moment as anything I'd seen. I doubt if they realised as they ground on toward Wexler Creek how sorry I was to see them go. Ron, Ellen and the guys, if you read this, I want you to know that our meeting meant more than almost anything to me at the time. I still have the blanket you sold me, which kept me warm at night. Also the carved wooden animal, which I stared at on later nights when I was living with the Veggies. What is it? I thought it was some kind of wild sheep, but the legs are too long. I'm afraid your stylistic conventions are strange to me, but it gave me something to count as I lay in my sleeping bag watching the living green numbers of the clock and waiting for the muttered whirrs of its unexpected and undesigned electrical storms. The clock belonged to Sandy Lorenzo, and he insisted, brightly and reasonably, that it observed total silence whenever he used it. It didn't even tick—there was scarcely anything mechanical in it at all. But he's young and always sleeps, so he wouldn't notice. He has no real problems except for being a sort of unofficial PR man and fixer for the Brainchildren (Associated Intellectual Interest Group) on campus.

Nevertheless, he is a nice guy, and the Veggies are nice girls, too. No doubt I would have had a lot of fun in that situation if I could only have known for certain that I was the one having it. Naturally I could have just picked a name out of the air, e.g. James Milliner Hubbard, one which seems to go well with my stocky, greying, bearded appearance, as noticed by me in a mirror outside Dean Overbird's office when I was going to be interviewed by him after my existence on campus had finally been taken note of. But the odds against any name being the right one are literally millions to one, so that to pick a name was always in practice to feel an impostor. At night I wrote long lists of names, eliminating all of them:

Aaronovitch
Abel
Abrahams
Abromsky
Acanthus
Ackroyd
Actifed etc.

And in Dean Overbird's office we discussed two more—Samuel Taylor Coleridge and Silas Tomken Cumberbatch. Sitting on rather than in a new leather armchair and surrounded by shiny new books, as if his image had just been renovated and perhaps years of grime scraped off his genial surfaces, the Dean told me of Silas Tomken Cumberbatch, the alias which the poet Coleridge had assumed when he ran away from Cambridge, England, and joined the army. Fortunately, his erudition displayed itself in his correction of an officer's quotation from Aeschylus, and he was sent back where he belonged. Coleridge had been a bad Trooper, and had let his musket go rusty. Dean Overbird laughed self-consciously and his eyes were sad behind a long nose. In return for this news I explained how

Sandy Lorenzo had arranged with Barb and Cheryl, the two Veggies who found me sleeping behind a rock and brought me home for purposes of their own, that I should be allowed to give poetry readings in the ADIG main recreation hall, that the first of these was planned for next Thursday at 8.30. And then he arranged an appointment for me with the university psychiatrist, a man in a small grey suit who seems to be all wrists and teeth, and not always the same teeth either, as he has a smile that can begin in any area of his mouth and never manages to occupy all of it at once.

'My friend,' he told me, 'you are in what psychologists call a fugue state.'

A fugue is a state that characterises certain types of neurotic crisis, a state in which the subject loses his memory and sense of identity and strikes out on the road for a new life. I remarked that the expression seemed to be a contradiction in terms, as one is either in a state or running away from it, but Dr Jespersen replied that life was essentially paradoxical and that, properly speaking, a fugue state was something one ran *through*, as I had run through part of Southern California and Nevada to get to Desert Greens. He said that I needed intensive therapy, which he would be willing to give if I made an appointment with him in two weeks. In the event this has not proved necessary, as my second wife, Eva Kohlrabi, took me to a sanatorium in Blue Mountain, which I am glad to say turned out to be of the pingpong rather than the electrotherapy type.

While waiting for this deliverance, there was nothing much to do except eat stewed pulses and brown rice, marvel at the changes that had taken place in the university system since my day (though at that time I wasn't sure I had had one) and enjoy the hospitality of Barb and Cheryl, who, by virtue of having found me asleep under a boulder one morning when they were walking in the desert looking for edible succulents, claimed certain rights in respect of me which I did not immediately find out about as they were a little shy. I lived in one corner of a sort of communal room where there was much coming and going of vegetarian women. Most Veggies seem to be female, also tall, stringy, pleasant to look at. Once, though, I had a long discussion with a male Veggie, a small boy with a big beard who confided that he'd really wanted to be a Wizard (Associated Magical Interest Group (Western)) but his powers of concentration hadn't been strong enough. He'd tried hard to meditate on the Tree of Life, but wasn't sure what colours the upper branches were meant to be, so he kept having to open his eyes and look at the picture again.

'That fucking pink Yesod,' he muttered, 'that threw me. I thought it was going to be all incense and virgins.' So he found himself among the Veggies where the sex life was assured and the qualifications for acceptance merely dietary. 'I fucked the Qabbalah,' he told me blasphemously. 'You might as well be a Brainchild.'

The motives which Barb and Cheryl had for bringing me back through the desert and installing me in a corner of that thoroughfare-like room were, I now realise, sexual. One night about a week later I woke from my hard-won sleep to find Cheryl kneeling on my stomach in one of those long Victorian nightgowns with floral decorations on them. 'Hey, Joe,' she said speculatively (it was as good a name as any), 'want me to do you a favour?'

She undid the zipper of my sleeping bag and started feeling about, keeping her eyes questioningly on my face the whole time. After a while she developed a sort of pleased look. Taking up position around the mid-thigh region she bent over the part that interested her, and for the next quarter of an hour I have only the memory of her yellow-brown hair swaying slightly and the white cotton shoulders hunched forward and little sucking noises coming from the direction of my loins. That was all she wanted—she left right after, and the next night it was Barb who came and did the same thing.

When Sandy came to see me a few days later I asked him about it. Sandy was elected BMOC (Big Man on Campus) last year for the second year running and this year he is going for a unique treble. Perhaps he is trying to compensate for his appearance, for he really *looks* like a Brainchild, with the blue eyes, large head and colourless hair of a two-year-old, and an underdeveloped body to match. He has a deep understanding of the complexities of campus life. His campaign for BMOC last year was based on a single letter, as his opponents said at the time. Unlike the other *Associated* Groups, the Christian Group at Desert Greens was known as *United* (United Christian Interest Group), an appellation that was calculated to make it a privileged faction. Sandy's campaign against this was backed by many of the Christians themselves, who felt their title was depriving them of the inalienable right to disagree with each other.

Anyway, when I asked him why Barb and Cheryl felt so strongly about blowjobs, he answered that fellatio performed a vital social function on campus. Sexual intercourse is still associated, however falsely, with notions of pair bonding and the meaningful relationship, while a kiss is something and nothing. Young people needed a kind of token sex whose meaning would be more diplomatic than passionate. 'For us, it's like a peace pipe,' he said, 'though naturally we have those as well.'

I said I had thought maybe they were suffering from some kind of protein deficiency. Sandy replied that in the strictest etymological sense the vegetarian diet is the only *radical* diet possible. To eat a steak is to exploit it, whereas a bean, unlike a bull, is not a worker but a product. Sandy shows a real sympathy for the ideals of other groups. At all events, these formal greetings, for they were little more than that, became an increasingly pleasant part of my life on campus and I was gradually able to persuade Barb and Cheryl to let some of the others join in. I found it very restful. It helped me get to sleep when the clock started playing up. And I wrote the girls a poem, which I planned to introduce into my show:

POEM

Night falls on campus with its cold
And desert landscapes of despair,
That dark discovery of the old.
Brightness, like Nash's, leaves the air,

And leaves are all that's left the night.
They shake between the vacant blocks
Of faculty. Their springtime blight
Is just the gnawing of the clocks,

Is just that time just won't stand still—
Hold still! You hold me as I lie,
You soothe the stiff revolt of will
And drink my straining demon dry.

All my poems are in the quatrain form. I learned later that I am a formalist and believe in order, craftsmanship and the lasting value of tradition. At the time iambic lines in little blocks of abab, cdcd etc, seemed the only facts or artefacts I could be sure of. They had an absolute individual value, as opposed to the relative social value put forward by Eva Kohlrabi in her confrontation with Dean Overbird.

'I need hardly say,' she said, 'that poetry is one of the oldest and most honourable of all the arts. My second husband's work has been published in leading magazines and journals on both sides of the Atlantic—even in *The Times Literary Supplement!* He has been poet-in-residence at the University of the Midwest, and has taught creative writing courses in five states.'

Dean Overbird, on the defensive against this onslaught, sensed the weakness of Eva's position. 'If you'll excuse me,

Mrs Kohlrabi, I fail to see why, even if your second husband is, as you put it, "hiding" on campus, I should take any steps to locate him for you. After all, what rights do you have in the matter? Assuming you are like most American women in holding husbands consecutively rather than concurrently and without wishing for a moment to interfere in your private life, surely it is Mr Kohlrabi you should be holding at the moment.'

'No healthy civilisation has existed,' she replied urgently, 'which did not also have a healthy poetry. Poetry is one of the lynchpins of culture. Surely you, Dean Overbird, as Dean of Arts and Sciences at this university, have some responsibility toward culture. My second husband is part of our heritage. He is a big man in the poetry world, and it is my duty to get him back.'

It was dark on campus, and people were beginning to gather outside the main recreation hall. Through the window I could see the orange robes of Hare Krishna monks affiliated to AMIG (Eastern) shining a pale, anonymous colour—notwhite. For the first time in many months, I laughed. They were all coming to see Anon, the man who wrote those jingly proverbial poems about the Western Wind and that kind of stuff. Inside, the hall looked like before or after a wedding, blank wooden space. Sandy was going round holding an empty blue plastic bong in his left hand and shaking hands with everybody with his right. After a while one of the Veggies thought of opening the main doors, and the atmosphere improved a little as the embarrassed groups in their variegated clothing moved in. Soon they were drinking, talking and smoking. I moved among the young people and the space around me moved also. I had the feeling that when I had found the right place to stand the show could begin, but nobody had told me where it was. Suddenly I heard a voice shout 'Order!' and I knew it was Sandy, although I couldn't see him. After some muttering the kids moved to the edges of the hall, leaving Sandy alone in the centre.

'You all know me,' he said. 'I've put on shows for you before and you haven't always liked them. No, not all of you. I've put on rock concerts and classical concerts, drama, folksong, anything I could get. Some of you liked it, some of you didn't. Now I've found something I think you'll all like. My friend is going to recite tonight—I won't say my friend Who because he doesn't have a name.' Applause. 'He's going to read some poems which are all he knows. You may think this is just academic and culture and only good for wiping your ass with, but they're the only real things in the world for him. He lives for them.'

There was a silence, which I thought was bewilderment. Looking round, I realised it was respect. They all wished— the neat ones, the ragged ones, the solid ones, the desperate ones, the devout ones and the agnostic ones—that they knew as little as I did. Wouldn't that be something?

The lights went out, and the author of *American Rubai'yat* was alone. Then there was a single spotlight on my face, and I saw that the students had closed in again. They stood or sat in groups of between two and ten, close together, sometimes intertwined. As I began to recite, the spot started to move (one of Sandy's ideas), so that I had to follow it, winding among the clustered figures briefly illuminated as part of their heritage passed uttering its dateless words of love and death:

POEM

My cherry's branches hide the streets.
It's mad for love now. Spring *is* so.
I reach upon the shelf for Keats,
Still centre of a world I know.

My hair is whiter than before.
My mistresses know less and less.
Blake's shining world I never saw.
I have seen gardens, and success,

But shall not find such trees again,
Though given Homer's sight, or mine
When I was twenty-one. What then
Shall my white brain incarnadine

When alien rhythms pound the ear?
The sidewalk's treasures shall be palling,
My lovelife trudged into the sere,
The yellow leaf. And poets falling.

There was a disturbing silence. In the loud youthful applause delivered with the feet as well as the hands that followed, I noticed that the main door was open again and as one of the bald men in orange clapped me on the back I became aware of a woman I knew but could not remember, who walked quickly up to me and introduced me to my audience in a clear, nervous voice. Somebody whistled, and somebody else said, 'His mistresses know more and more,' and there was a big laugh. The Dean took my other arm, and they walked me carefully out of the hall. As we were leaving, brightness and levity descended on its occupants. I heard one boy say, 'Never heard of the guy,' and others agreed.

'Where in hell do you find these people, Sandy?' asked someone, and Sandy smiled. That boy is going to make a name for himself some day.

The Lovers

They were not of an Age but for all Time, the motto says in English and Greek on the stained-glass window adorned with images of six writers of each nationality: on one side the heads of Chaucer, Malory and Jonson surmounting full figures of Spenser, Shakespeare and Milton, on the other, Aeschylus, Euripides, Sophocles, Plato, Homer, Aristotle. The fifth-formers sit in the front row, the sun shining through Shakespeare's brown scalp into their eyes, while the headmaster declaims from the stage with the sixth form massed behind him, twisting his hands in his gown behind his back and staggering slightly as he always does, even when standing still.

'I am very sorry to have to tell you.' He has a way of saying words one at a time, so the announcement sounds like: 'the (death) of our (much-valued) (friend) and (fellow)-(pupil) (David) (Nisbet) in a (bicycle) (accident)'.

There is a little gasp, more for the sake of politeness than anything. It's Monday morning and Nisbet died on Saturday; most of the people who know or care who he was have already heard about it. The only part that's news to anyone is the bicycle accident, which is embarrassing: the sort of jolly, innocent death an adult would make up for a schoolboy. Did he even have a bike? None of them has ever visited his house on the other side of London so they have no idea.

There is a minute's silence so the school can listen to the rustles of its own discomfort, the squeaks of chair legs on the floor, a squawk of wind in one of the organ pipes. Sam Gregory, the fixer, neat and sandy-haired, looks across at Millgreen, sitting half a row away to the right, taller than the boys around him, an expression of suitable but not excessive emotion on his face. He is a classicist, who believes that man's natural instincts are dangerous and need to be kept in check by social constraints. He also has what he calls a

31

betrothed back home in Chiswick. Next to him is Walfisch, the hierophant, who looks, with his heavy-set body and large stubbled face, like a man in his forties, and is sometimes taken for one of the masters. Walfisch says he's above sex and his only lust is for knowledge. The three of them must have been the nearest thing to friends that Nisbet had. None of them could be said to feel grief, but it's still hard to believe. He wasn't serious enough for death, surely? It makes you think: if Nisbet can die there is no minimum qualification.

Millgreen feels that the day should be marked somehow; he has already decided not to attend choir practice this evening. He will be taking the day off to go to the funeral on Friday, as the whole form has been given permission to do, but he is not looking forward to it. He knows he will have to talk to Nisbet's mother there, Ursula as he must call her. He imagines her as tall and stately, her face whitened and stiffened by grief so that it looks like a bust of Athene; he doesn't think she will cry, judging by her voice on the phone to him the other night, but if she does it will be in an unconvulsive, sobless way, the tears slipping out and down in spite of herself. This he can stand. What worries him is the thought that she will come up to him and clutch his arm, kiss him, draw him to her body in an embrace that he will be too courteous to detach himself from. And then it will be too late—she will believe for ever that he was Nisbet's friend, may even want to see him on other occasions, and he will never be able to tell her, yes, I knew him, we played chess sometimes, he used to phone me every Sunday night at eleven to find out what the English prep was for Monday morning, but that is all. Millgreen believes in telling the truth, but the time to do that was on Saturday when he was too shocked by the news, by the whole situation. From the moment his mother called him into the hall to tell him there was a lady on the phone for him he knew there was something wrong.

'Is that Gideon?'

'Yes.'

'This is Ursula Nisbet speaking. David's mother.'

Already his mind was struggling to catch up, to remind him that Nisbet carried on existing on Saturday nights out there in Grove Park with his full name and his mother, leading his ununiformed life. And this cool, milky voice was part of it, flowed round Nisbet all through his off-hours. The thought was so unnerving he hardly noticed what she was saying.

'I'm afraid I've got some bad news. David died suddenly today.'

The way she said *died suddenly* made it sound as if it was one of those things that happened in life, like one's voice breaking. Which David were they talking about again?

'I thought you would like to know.'

A hint that he was supposed to reply. 'Yes, thank you, that's very kind of you.' He tried to put warmth in his voice to show how grateful he was.

'I found your number in his address-book,' the voice said. Millgreen's reply was obviously the wrong one, because it had become slightly harder and more formal, explaining itself. 'So I decided to call you.'

'Oh yes, thank you.'

'Would you let his other friends know for me?'

'Of course, um, Mrs Nisbet. I'm sorry. I really am very sorry.'

'Ursula,' she said. 'I know you are. Thank you, Gideon. That means so much to me.'

She rang off without giving him time to explain that the number was in Nisbet's address-book because of Sunday night prep. And now his supposed friendship with her son is some kind of bond between them. Millgreen is pacing up and down the cloisters, trying to think. Although the playground, with its screaming first-formers is just a few

33

yards away, no one is allowed to run here. He queues at one of the drinking fountains and crouches over it thirstily, ignoring the piece of chewing gum stuck to the nozzle; the water is ice-cold, chlorine-tasting, piped, according to an age-old rumour, from the swimming pool. He wonders if he is ill—isn't excessive thirst supposed to be a symptom of diabetes? Standing, he puts his hand on his forehead. It feels hot, but then, as he reminds himself, if he did have a temperature it would affect the hand as well as the head. He might use that idea in the English essay he's writing: to see the individual as the source of moral values makes as much sense as trying to take your temperature with your hand. Values can only come from a community. He looks round the cloisters and sighs. Not the kind of community he would have chosen to take his values from, assuming that the choice, paradoxically, had been up to him. Being large, he has always been selected for the rugby team and the athletics throwing events, both of which he hates. While he excels in class, he receives from the masters an almost subliminal message that his particular brand of excellence has something unsavoury about it. It's as if they secretly want him to charge around the corridors knocking people over, to forget his prep from time to time and even to answer back. How do you conform to an institution that demands insubordination?

There were no such problems for Nisbet, who was in detention every Tuesday and Friday without fail. Millgreen couldn't help admiring the barefacedness of his approach: no lies about leaving the prep on the train, just a straightforward Ah, sir, there you have me. 'Why don't you just do it, Nisbet?' he asked him over one of their chess games.

'Er, good question.'

'It wasn't a rhetorical one.'

But Nisbet only smirked and crouched lower over his battered pocket set where two of the black pawns had been

34

replaced by matchsticks. If he could be said to be serious about anything, it was chess. He carried magazines in his pocket and would produce one in the course of a game to check he was following the opening correctly. When Millgreen pointed out that this was cheating, he protested that the openings were all known anyway, so there was no skill in playing them. The real game began once you were *out of the book*. Millgreen knew nothing about chess beyond the moves and the notion that anyone should read books on it seemed criminally frivolous to him.

'Ponziani's Opening,' Nisbet announced. 'It's not very sound.'

He believed that he had one great game in him and always at some point raised a finger in the air and, said 'Aha!' under the temporary delusion that this might be the one. He was quite prepared to have his brilliant winning sacrifice reclassified as comedy when it turned out not to work.

Millgreen wandered round Room 27A talking about Heraclitus and Anaximander, eating an apple, stopping sometimes to pick up a dictionary from the bookshelves so that he could look up the etymology of some word that had taken his interest and only coming back to the board when it was his turn to move. 'And if you're not going to do it,' he persisted, 'why go to the trouble of phoning me to find out what it is?'

'So I'll know what I haven't done?' Nisbet looked up at him hopefully to see if he had made a joke.

'The masters set the prep to help you to learn. Plato says that every man finds pleasure in learning. It is the nature of humankind. Apart from which, they just give you a detention when you don't.'

'Tell me about your fiancée.'

'What about her?'

'Well, has she got a name?'

'Her name is Rachel. We've known each other since childhood.'

'And you really are engaged?'

'I intend to marry her when we reach twenty-one, yes.'

'Does she know it?'

'We have, an understanding.'

'And do you kiss her and…' Nisbet squirmed over the chess set. 'Feel her up?'

'I don't want to talk about her in that way, if you don't mind.' Millgreen regretted sounding so prim, but what else could he say?

'Is she pretty?'

'No, but she is beautiful. To me.'

'Don't you ever fancy other women?'

'You mean do I ogle the secretaries in Pyramid House? Do I press myself against blondes on the Tube during the rush hour? Do I keep copies of *Mayfair* in my desk? No, I don't. Because it's only pampering the animal in yourself, which will never be happy until it has consumed your reason. I intend to get married, Nisbet, because marriage is an institution specifically designed to give the animal a neat and well-tended pasture to graze in.'

'If I had a fiancée,' Nisbet said, 'I don't know what I'd do with her.'

Or did he say, 'I know what I'd do with her'? Now that it might be important, Millgreen isn't sure. And with a shock he remembers that Nisbet actually met Rachel shortly after that, the night she came to hear him sing in *Elijah*. They were walking arm-in-arm here in the cloisters, which had been turned into a refreshment area for the occasion, with trestle tables laid out with ham and cheese sandwiches, pink and green marshmallows and tall frothing glasses of ice cream soda. In the archways, diagonal streaks of rain showed bronze in the lights, and sometimes a gust of wind would swish some of it inside, causing shrieks and giggles from the girlfriends and mothers. Millgreen was off-duty now, tired and triumphant from the singing, Rachel in a flowery dress pressing softly against him as he steered her

36

through the crowds. And suddenly there was Nisbet, brushed and in a suit, shaking hands with Rachel, putting his head on one side to smile at her: 'Charmed to meet you, madam.' And Millgreen pulled her away sharply, calling out a quick goodbye over his shoulder. He could hardly have been jealous of Nisbet. But he had seen a flash of something pass between them that he felt, obscurely, he must protect him from.

Now he knows it was too late. He pictures Nisbet in his room, an attic one, surrounded by chess books and unwashed clothes. (No doubt he refused to allow Ursula in there more than once a week.) He must have lain on his bed, staring at the cobwebs on the beams, dreaming of Rachel's white arms, straight nose, long, almost-blonde hair, thinking up jokes he might have told her if they had been allowed to talk to each other, that he might still tell her if he ever managed to meet her again. Hopeless. At least if Nisbet had been Keats or Shelley he could have written poems about it, pernicious ones in Millgreen's opinion, but it might have saved his life. As it is—what is the romantic's way to commit suicide? Not slashing your wrists in the bath: that would be too heroically classical. No, he reaches for a bottle on the shelf, paracetamol, untwists the cap, takes out the cotton wool from the neck...

And Rachel has no idea of the deed she has inspired. He can never explain and she would probably not understand if he tried. As a matter of fact, he hasn't seen Rachel for a couple of weeks, not since she was so offhand when he asked her to come to the Palestrina at the Royal Festival Hall. Chocolate and earrings and the activities of various friends from her school, some of them male, are her principal interests these days. There are times when he wonders if they do have an understanding after all. But he hasn't talked to anyone about what's happened, unless you count Ursula, and he feels the event ought to be marked in some way. If he's not going to tell Rachel, perhaps he will drop into church on his way home and say a prayer for Nisbet's soul. There is no God, but at times it is necessary to behave as if there is, for the sake of a well-ordered mind.

At lunchtime, one of the secretaries in Pyramid House, the massive office building on the far side of the playground, breaks her kettle and shouts down to Sam to ask if he can fix it. He has had his eye for months on a girl who works on the same floor, the one who wears the blue sweater, so he shouts back: 'Sure, why not?' She lowers the kettle carefully on a string, past window after window where other secretaries and their managers must be looking up from their desks to see it go by. Halfway down, the lid comes off; it doesn't fall straight, but spins and tumbles like an unbalanced frisbee, taking the wind and spiralling off to land with a clang about fifty yards away in the middle of a football game being played with a tennis ball. (School rules, to encourage ball-control skills and minimise breakage of windows.)   He takes hold of the kettle and the girl looks down from her window, a face fringed with limp hair. 'Probably a broken element,' he shouts, and the hair nods, then withdraws. I'm in there, Sam thinks gloomily. What's her name? Gemma, isn't it? There was a time when he knew most of the girls in Pyramid House, at least to shout to and gesture at, but that was when they were still a challenge. It has been getting him down recently, the thought that all the fanciable women in the world are older than him. They're called girls, even he calls them girls, when they have jobs and bank accounts and cars, and most of them are taller. You can kiss them all you want, but it doesn't take away the fact that you have to wear a black blazer with a gold badge and a black and red stripy tie and that hair is to be worn short of the collar. Maybe that's why he fancies the blue-sweater girl, who has never asked him to take a look at her brake-pads or sell her a quarter of an ounce of Moroccan hash. If he's going to be a schoolboy for another two and a half years, he might as well find a woman that treats him like one. Though, to be fair, she's never taken any notice of him, so can't be said to be treating him as anything.

Sam is in the cellars by now sorting through a pile of old kettle elements, trying to find one that fits. Nobody knows this space like he does, certainly not the school caretakers, who confine themselves to a little corner of it underneath the kitchens. He has rigged up a lab-cum-workroom of his own here, complete with a buzzing, unsteady electricity supply run off from the school's main generator and his own power tools. It is here he does the repair work that helps keep him in drugs and cigarettes, making a charge for all customers with a Y chromosome.

He'll say one thing for Nisbet—he was easily impressed. Sam remembers him standing here, gazing round with his dull green eyes, trying to think of something clever to say. 'Aha!' he said in the end, raising a forefinger, 'an electrical current!' And opened and closed his mouth several times. He was trying to work out a pun, but was too poleaxed to manage it.

'What a shock?' Sam suggested, trying to put him at ease.

'Ah,' Nisbet agreed. In the undiffused bulblight, his cheeks looked redder than ever as he turned slowly round looking for something to sit on, failing to find it then turning round all over again. He would have carried on revolving indefinitely if Sam hadn't found him an unopened catering-size cardboard box of teabags that bowed under the pressure of his buttocks but didn't split. Nisbet was the first person Sam had ever brought here. He didn't even bring his girls—Pyramid House provided plenty of after-hours office space to cavort in and it always gave him a thrill to look up from the warm neck of a secretary and see the gothic bulk of the blacked-out school on the other side of the glass.

Everyone else was too cool or too embarrassed to ask Sam, 'How do you manage it?' Nisbet took his time getting there, though. He started coming up to him in Room 27A when no

39

one was about, waving his forefinger and saying, 'Mr Gregory, I presume.' Sam had no idea what he was after. And then one day, 'What a gay dog you are,' Nisbet said, and while Sam was wondering whether it would be necessary to punch him in the mouth, added with a triumphant little cough and a flourish of the forefinger, 'I don't mean that in the vulgar modern sense, of course.' It turned out Nisbet had been staying late, watching what he got up to in Pyramid House. 'You are, ahem, something of a ladies' man, I think.' The funny thing was, Sam had never thought of himself in those terms; Nisbet wanted some tips and tricks and, as far as he knew, Sam didn't have any.

'I don't know, I just kind of, wave at them.'

'Wave at them?'

'And you know, shout.'

'Shout? What kind of things do you shout?'

'Oh, anything. Lovely weather we're having, like the new hair, what you doing later?'

'All three things at once, or one at a time?'

'I don't know, Nisbet. It doesn't really matter what the words are. Anything will do. You just talk to them. Only louder, because they're a long way away.'

Nisbet's lips moved, practising the lines. Just be yourself, Sam was about to say, and then it occurred to him that being himself would be fatal in this case. Imagine him standing at the formroom window waving his finger in the air and shouting 'Aha!' at the sweater-girl, or even at Gemma. You are something of a lady, I presume. If he was going to act naturally, he was going to have to be taught.

'Listen,' Sam told him in the cellar, 'the first thing you have to do is sort out your appearance. I've got a mirror here somewhere.' It was a round dressing-table type with magnifying glass on one side, still in its box underneath a pile of stereo equipment, and when he finally found it, the dim-harsh light of his bulb was hardly adequate for Nisbet to see the extent of the problem. All the veins in his cheeks seemed to be broken, as if by some catastrophic embarrassment in his past. The nose, similarly, had a broken look, and gave the face a permanent sadness, which the smirk of the mouth turned into a parody of glee. You could at least change that. 'Try not to smile, Nisbet, OK?'

'I'm not smiling.'

His hair had probably never been combed, and when Sam produced his silver-plated comb in its leather sheath, sharp enough to draw blood, he didn't know what to do with it. 'Do you have a parting? Do you have a fringe?'

'I have hair,' Nisbet said.

The clothes were worse: the blazer that was so big he looked as if he had a second, higher pair of shoulders inside the first, the un-ironed shirt with one wing of the collar up and the other down, the tie with the narrow end protruding six inches below the wide end. 'All girls want from a man,' Sam told him, 'is to look as though you happened on purpose.'

Now, sitting in his cellar with the kettle at his feet, he has the depressing thought that maybe nobody does happen on purpose. Does he have any more control than Nisbet had? The only thing those lessons achieved was to make Sam feel superior; they did nothing for Nisbet, who didn't get his hair cut and carried on dressing the same way. So why had he asked for them—did he actually want to feel worse about himself? Or did he want to be reassured that there was an alternative mode of being, if he could only be bothered to adopt it?

But then there was the night when Sam came into Room 27A and found him staring at the blue-sweater girl. It was that peculiar time between the end of after-school activities (detentions, play rehearsals, Combined Cadet Force, Fencing Club) and the locking of the main gate. Elsewhere the early evening news was starting, but here it was already midnight: the lights were turned out in the nave-like corridors and the formrooms were shadowy and smelled of disinfectant. He

41

opened the door and saw Nisbet sitting on top of a desk by the open window, his feet drawn up, staring out across the darkness at the girl, who was not wearing her blue sweater tonight, but a crimson blouse. She looked as if she was about to go out on the town; standing unnoticed in the doorway, Sam couldn't see down far enough, but the way she was moving suggested high heels. She was alone in the office, busy with what was probably a last-minute tidy-up and put-away. He knew how prosaic the doings were in that building, monthly sales figures and cost-effectiveness studies, but some magical property of glass turned her movements into a solitary druidic ceremony. Nisbet never took his eyes off her and his face, for the first time ever, wasn't wearing that smile. We both love her, Sam realised—even he knows this is not just another lady. And at that moment the crimson-bloused woman turned and stood full-on, facing the window. She looked, not at Sam in his corner, but straight at Nisbet. Then, with a semicircular sweep of her arm, she waved at him, once, twice, three times. Sam's eyes went straight to Nisbet to see what he would do, wave back, jump up and open the window, shout something. But he stayed motionless, his expression unchanging. There was no one else she could have been waving at. Maybe he thought she was getting back at him for staring. No, her eyes were wide and serious and the wave was too purposeful, heavy with semaphore-like meaning. Sam had been on the end of a few signals himself, could remember the first time he'd received one of those looks, the way his stomach had turned over. He almost went up to Nisbet and shook him, screamed in his ear, she wants to meet you, you arsehole, go and get her– *almost*, that is, in the sense of *not at all*. The girl's wave had paralysed both of them, Nisbet on the desk and Sam in the doorway, and she seemed to be satisfied by that, because she gave a little nod, then turned away, got her coat from a stand by the door and left the office. And Sam slipped away too, leaving Nisbet staring into the illuminated space as if he thought there was still a person in it to look at.

Every day Nisbet had to sit in class knowing that she was there on the other side of the playground, cool blue or hot scarlet, whatever, waiting in that glass case for him to go across to her. In his stripy tie and his non-fitting blazer. It must have driven him mad to have the adult world staring right back at him, out of reach, and this weekend he just—

Crap: he's knocked a whole stack of Japanese microwaves on to the concrete floor. What's he wasting his time for? He's got a job to do, hasn't he?

Nisbet will never make a ghost, Walfisch thinks. After all, if everyone became a ghost when they died, the world would be overpopulated with them. It takes intense spiritual and mental focus to qualify for the afterlife. All that stuff about headless horsemen and the spirits of murdered women crying out for revenge, that's what causes the confusion. There is nothing sensational about ghosts. Usually they don't have bodies, and when they do there's no dripping blood. For the dead, the material world is as vague and wispy as their world is to us, and a lot less interesting. The only reason they deign to appear here at all is when they have a message to pass on. Another common misconception: that they come back to tell us where the buried treasure is, or that we mustn't get the number 14 bus to work tomorrow or even that they still love us. They have different priorities now. Love and money don't mean anything to them and as for warning us we might be about to get killed, why should that seem a problem to someone who's dead already? Walfisch has had dozens of messages from the dead, and none of them made any sense.

So he is not worried that Nisbet's ghost holds him responsible. Nisbet has dissolved into the Æther, his red cheeks and green eyes just part of the swirling patterns in the universal fluid. Walfisch realises that he has been staring at the blotches of light made by the stained-glass windows on the rows of blue plastic stacking chairs down below, inadvertently projecting his thoughts into the shimmering colours. He is sitting in the organ loft above the Great Hall, the place where he gives his tarot readings. Apart from morning assembly, it is only ever used for organ lessons on Thursdays, so he can be sure of privacy here, and he finds the vertigo and echoing space conducive to a spiritual atmosphere. Not that it had that effect on Nisbet.

'The Fool! How dare you, sir!' He gave a waggle of the finger, as if thinking of stabbing Walfisch with it.

'The Fool is your Significator. He represents your innermost self.'

'Ha! Insult me, would you?'

'Do not underestimate the Fool. He is Jesus and Dionysus, the incarnation of our highest and most self-sacrificing nature. He smells a rose even as he steps over a cliff. His mind is on immaterial things.'

Looking back, Walfisch tries to remember if there was any clue in the cards. Nothing obvious, certainly, like Death or the Ten of Swords. But The Lovers turned up—he remembers Nisbet getting excited over the naked figures: 'Oh look, a lady in her birthday suit!'

Why did he ask for a reading in the first place if he wasn't going to take it seriously? He must have been after something, but it didn't seem like it at the time. The reading was never finished—instead, Nisbet grabbed the cards when the Tree of Life was only half-laid-out, with a shout of 'My deal!'

A shame, because he had the makings of an acolyte. There was a pained look in the eyes that suggested spiritual depths behind the frivolity. 'You know, Nisbet,' Walfisch said, 'there are other worlds than this. What happens here is only a reflection, a shimmer on the surface of the universe.'

Nisbet put down the cards. 'Can you do magic?'

'Indeed. I can hold converse with the dead, and with what you would call Angels. I can foretell the future, at times. I can fly in my sleep. I can make myself invisible when I choose.'

'How do you make yourself invisible?'

'It is not a party trick. It takes years of study and practice.'

'But when did you start? You're only...'

'Fifteen, of your years.'

'And people can see right through you?'

'It's more that they don't look at me. It amounts to the same thing.'

'What about these angels you talk to?'

How to explain to someone like that the orders of Angels and Dæmons? There is so much that even Walfisch doesn't know and far more that he knows but dare not reveal. But however it was, he told Nisbet too much, one evening a few weeks later, when they got talking in Room 27A and he found himself explaining about the succubus. 'The name comes from *sub*, under, and *cubere*, to lie: a spirit that lies under, a female spirit that has sex with men. There is also the incubus, a male spirit that has sex with women.' Walfisch has always thought it significant that *us* is a masculine ending in Latin—the succubus is not really female, for it is not alive.

'You mean, you can do it with a ghost?' Nisbet said.

'Believe me, you wouldn't want to try it. It's pleasant at first, but... The succubus is a sort of psychic disease. You catch it, if you're very unlucky.'

'What from?'

'There are spirits which lie around waiting to be picked up. There's a story, for example, of a nun who swallowed a Dæmon that was sitting on a lettuce leaf. There may be a succubus in this very room, lying on a shelf or in a dusty corner. Then again, Eliphas Levi tells us that there are succubi that live in books. Read a certain word on a certain page and the succubus slips in through your eye into your brain.'

Nisbet was redder in the face than usual, breathing hard, too excited to say anything flippant. Perhaps he was infected already, with the *desire* to be infected. It was harmless enough, surely, to tell him about it? After all, what were the chances of him actually encountering one?

But if the succubus feeds on sexual desire, where better for it to lurk than in the midst of seven hundred and fifty adolescent boys? The psychic energy in this building is immense, with only a handful of human females to channel it or, more probably, intensify it further: three or four teachers whose breasts get stared at irrespective of their age or looks, and two girls who have been allowed into the sixth form to do Greek A level, one small and plump with frizzy hair, the other small and plump with straight hair. If you walk down the sixth-form corridor during break you will see the entire sixth form crammed into one or other of the rooms, standing or squatting on the desks, with the two girls holding audience in the middle. (The frizzy-haired one, to judge by her expression, is enjoying herself, while the straight-haired one isn't.) Open any desk, and you'll find, nestling among dried sandwich crumbs, dead insects, set squares and protractors, a dirty magazine or two, or a novel called something like *French Undressing* or *Heavy Petshop*. Most of them are new and trashy, but occasionally you come across an old book with stiff textbook-like covers and sprightly little line drawings or black-and-white photographs from the era when women always looked like cakes, even when naked. Lust has been building up here for a hundred years. At night when everyone has gone home, the formrooms and corridors flicker and crackle with it, a liquid, purplish light that only Walfisch, who has passed beyond sex, can see. Sooner or later, something had to ignite.

Nisbet must have found the secret. Perhaps it was in one of the pornographic novels or in one of those leather-bound gold-tooled books locked away behind glass in the library. He could have stolen the keys and stayed late reading, night after night, until he reached the fatal page and the virus took root. Or perhaps the succubus just smelled his need and made her own way to him down the corridors.

She would appear at first as a dream, the courtesan dancing for the sultan or the leather-clad strippergram, or someone quite innocent, the girl who sits next to you in the cinema and accidentally drops her choc ice on the front of your trousers and then tries to wipe it off with her fingers, and you think, that's funny, ice-cream is meant to be cold isn't it, and then you wake up with the alarm clock showing three-thirty and a lot of mopping up to do before you can go back to sleep. Nothing unusual about that. And then, after a few weeks, you reach the stage where the dream becomes less like a dream, and the girl less like a girl, when every time you go to bed, you know you'll be lying in the arms of that plasma that hasn't actually got arms, or breasts, or vagina, shaking and coming till there's nothing left to come but your vital substance, your soul. And all the time he must have carried on going to school, pale, flushed and listless, and nobody noticed the difference until the life in him was used up.

Everyone knows fifteen-year-old boys don't have bicycle accidents. At fifteen, the only thing that can kill you is love.

Demonland

Oposso, the 'civilised' southern tip of Kuovala. I lay on my hotel bed, unable to sleep because of the clatter of the electric fan and a visit I had just had from two members of President Le Bouquin's secret police. I was reading a book by Julian, an esoteric computer textbook about demons and debugging techniques:

> When a demon is enabled, it fires. If enabled while another demon is in the process of firing, however, it must wait for the prior demon to finish. A demon may be temporarily disabled in order to allow another demon to fire, but only three demons may be held in store in a disabled state at any one time. If several demons having equal priorities are enabled at the same time, they are executed in an arbitrary order and then disabled...

Clattering words. Somehow the two policemen who called on me that night had got hold of Julian's book, and wanted to know about it, about him. They already knew he had disappeared. Quite possibly he was in one of their own dungeons, telling everything he knew about disablement and arbitrary executions. Or possibly not. Perhaps they wanted to find him as much as I did. At any rate, the fact that he was an intellectual who wrote books they couldn't understand marked him down as a potential subversive in their eyes. They were nervous, pompous little men who had grafted a layer of CIA American on to their clanging Kuovalan accents. They had apparently taken the stuff about demons personally—'What is demon, hey? You know demons?'

A new sound competed with the fan now, a soft whooping like that of a swanee whistle. It was the girasol, or north wind, which had blown every night since my arrival in Kuovala a week before. The local people believe it carries the voices of spirits exiled for terrible crimes to the inhospitable north of the island, inhabited only by Communist guerrillas and naked Stone Age villagers. It was the same solemn whistling that woke me on my first night here; Murgh lay beside me, breathing hard as if running in her sleep from the imaginary spirits. A strand of black hair across her face flickered and trembled. 'Julian,' she murmured, 'Julian…' and rolled over.

Next morning she denied it. She was only what the Kuovalans call a jazz girl, very elegant and very ignorant, who made her living from the American oilmen and construction engineers of Smith and Van Allen. That first evening, she had floated on to the next bar stool, smiled and said, 'I Murgh,' with such simple assurance that I thought for a moment it was a verb. A girl like that could easily have known Julian—probably she knew several—but it was strange, all the same, that she should murmur anyone's name in her sleep. Except her own: 'I Murgh…'

Julian was my employee, a nomadic programmer who wandered all over the world advising customers on how to get the best out of their computer systems. At the time he disappeared he was working for Strom's, an engineering firm who were trying to build a road between Smith and Oposso in the face of great and typically Kuovalan difficulties. Strom's, in common with most of our customers, had liked Julian; he was so nervous, shaggy and unpunctual that he would have seemed like a brilliant programmer even if he hadn't actually been one. Brilliant he certainly was, but not dangerous, surely? Why should Le Bouqin or anyone else want Julian to disappear?

> The best way to eradicate bugs is by a system of
> prophylaxis. When bugs become aware that they
> will not be tolerated, they seldom develop. The

ideal bugless program would be one that contained no code at all. In view of the impossibility of this, programmers would do best to aim at a state of *virtual codelessness*.

At some point while reading Julian's book, I must have fallen asleep, but it didn't seem to make any difference. The words kept on spinning through my head, relentless in their meaninglessness, like the clattering of the electric fan, like the voices of the spirits in the girasol.

The grim Norwegian project manager knew all about bugs, though he pronounced them 'bogs'.

'Is all focking bogs,' he told me, 'bogs and focking yongle.' We ate corned beef curry with coconut milk in a tin hut whose walls shook and rang with the heat and the project manager talked with monotonous fatalism about the three years he had spent in the yongle. Oddly, there is no real jungle in Kuovala, only a rocky Pacific *maquis* full of thorns and tough roots, of bright poisonous flowers that look like insects and insects that look like flowers. The project manager had two hundred men scheduled to do two years' work in the next six months. Of these two hundred, seventeen had dysentery, six gonorrhoea and two had run off to join the Communists. After lunch, he took me to look at the road; dizzy with heat, chilli and singing tin walls, I followed him along two miles of smouldering asphalt, first smooth, then cracked by vines and creepers. At the end of the road, we stood and watched a blue butterfly palpitate on a branch. Only twelve miles beyond it was Oposso. Shadows shivered and leaves buzzed between us and the Kuovalan equivalent of civilisation.

'Did Julian seem worried to you?'

'He was always worried, you know. He was serious man, thinking always a lot. Very good at bogs.'

'He wrote a book about them.'

'*Demons and Debogging Techniques*. I have one in the hot. Is impossible to onderstand.'

The butterfly was about the size of a sparrow, but absurdly fragile. It appeared preoccupied, as if eating something on the branch, but there was nothing it could be eating. The project manager told me about the 'yazz girl' who had hung around with Julian for several days before he disappeared.

'He was not a kind of man for women, you know, only for bogs, and she didn't speak English. He sat on a rock writing programs, and she would be stroking his hair.'

There had been two pimps as well, little men who looked like Kuovalans but talked like Americans and asked a lot of questions. The project manager thought Julian hadn't taken much notice of them; he was too busy worrying about bugs.

Bugs, I thought, how could anyone not worry about bugs in an island like this? As if worrying about that shivering, buzzing twelve miles of yongle would turn it into Chiswick High Road. The butterfly was within a few inches of my face. When I reached out a finger, very gently, to touch it, it gave a tiny shudder and bit me.

Julian's demons fluttered round my bed. They had long tapering heads which made them look as though they were wearing night-caps and they changed colour continually: red, flame-yellow, butterfly blue. One carried a machine gun, which it fired at my head in brief, malicious bursts. (I learned to recognise it and to flinch when it approached.) Occasionally a demon was disabled. When this happened, it would flutter wearily to the floor, where it lay twitching until it was re-enabled. President Le Bouquin stood in the shadows, a bald, brown-skinned presence in khaki, smiling to himself.

'You wake,' said Murgh. She was sitting on the bed in the half-darkness.

'How long have I been here?'

She held up three fingers.

'Three what? Days? Weeks?'

But she didn't answer. 'You bit butterfly,' she told me.

'Yes, I remember. Where am I?'

'This Smith. Doctor soon.'

When the doctor did call, there was something ominous about his expression that made me ask him suddenly if I was dying.

'Slowly, like the rest of us,' he replied with a forced chuckle. He was one of those Edwardian Americans, a tall, bald man with a curling moustache and a deep, thoughtful voice. Whatever he was worried about, he hid it well.

That evening, I found Julian's book beside my bed. I had another try at it, but with no success. Like the little men who had called at the hotel that evening and whom I equated (wrongly?) with the two pimps who had hung around the Strom's construction site while the yazz girl stroked Julian's hair, I kept taking his bugs and demons personally. They had made an appearance in my dreams, after all. As I read, I assigned to each of them a pinched little Kuovalan face; like a novelist, I tried to discover the motive behind their actions. They must have some reason for all this enabling and disabling, this firing and executing, I thought, otherwise why do it? Of course, in my saner moments I was aware that there was no motive, only the logic of the program.

Next morning the camp was in a panic that nobody tried to hide. Through the walls of the hut I could feel people running about with a random urgency so unceasing and desperate that it was exhausting to listen to. At lunchtime, the doctor told me that I was to be moved to Van Allen right away. Eventually he admitted that there were rumours of a Communist raid on Smith. The government had been alerted and had promised to send troops along the coast road via Van Allen, but no one knew when they would arrive.

'You'll be safer in Van Allen,' the doctor said. 'You're still suffering some residual toxaemia as a result of the butterfly, but there's no reason why you shouldn't travel. A sick man will only be a liability here and it wouldn't be good for your health to be shot at.'

'Nor for yours,' I told him, but he shrugged and replied that you couldn't dismantle a whole oilfield even if you wanted to. So after lunch they put me on a stretcher, and two Kuovalan labourers carried me along a sickening bumpy road that got further and further from Smith without getting nearer to anywhere else. Shadows shivered, leaves buzzed, but I could no longer tell whether they were inside my head or outside. From time to time I would call out to the labourers to ask them how much further, but they trudged on silently like mummies in a horror film as the sweat stains slowly darkened their T-shirts.

By the time I realised they were taking me to the Communists I was too ill to care.

For many days I sat as if hypnotised on the floor of the cave in which I was being held prisoner. I was CIA vampire, worm on hide of popular state, chap who dared defy will of Kuovala People's Marxist Socialist Army. At mealtimes I ate dried saltfish curry and drank Kuovalan bottled beer with its alarming petrol-and-blackberries taste. At night the fire threw big military shadows on the wall of the cave and I imagined they were President Le Bouquin's men come to rescue me. But nobody came except specially selected soldiers with recantations for me to sign. The recantations were difficult to understand, but I signed all of them. They bore the name G.L Fredora, either as a letter heading or underneath the text, as the names of company directors appear on business stationery.

'Julian imperialist traitor, is it?' my guard said eagerly when I asked him. 'We knowing very well.' Apparently Julian had lived in the camp for several weeks and had seemed willing to join them permanently, though he was still, even in the absence of a computer, preoccupied with his bugs. Suddenly, however, he had disappeared; the guard was still quite bitter about it. I supposed Julian must have left Strom's in a hurry to get away from the secret police, but why had he left the Communists and where was he now? Perhaps they had caught up with him.

I had noticed Murgh in the camp the day I arrived. She was sitting with a group of women in fatigues, caps and cartridge belts, looking as if she had been there all her life. In due course she appeared, wearing an impressive air of military severity and waving another recantation. When I had signed it, she sighed at me in a headmistressy way and said, 'You go home.'

'What do you mean?'

'You go, you go home. If.'

'You mean England?'

'Mean.'

'Can you get me out of the camp?'

'I sleep Fredora.'

'Murgh, where is Julian?'

'Not Julian.'

'You know where he is, don't you, Murgh? Everywhere I go, you're there first.'

'If you go. Then you go home. Not looking Julian. Else stay. Therefore!'

She spoke the last word potently, like an obscenity.

There are many obscenities in the Kuovalan language. If I had stayed long enough, I might have been able to compile a dictionary of them. 'Therefore' is certainly one, as are 'if', 'else' and 'because'. These are words specifically reserved for the demons of their ancient religion, which have their chief shrine hundreds of feet below the Communist camp.

The cave of the demons is a large, enclosed space like an orchestra pit, the music provided by a small waterfall that falls on to the stone floor from high up in the cave wall. The stone is porous; the water runs right through it, leaving no trace except a black glossiness. Vala lives in this cave, brooding about the island that is named after him. His personification is a pastel wall-painting twenty feet high, pot-bellied, shark-toothed, nightcap-headed. Around him, bugs and minor demons, even my own poisonous blue butterfly, scowl and flutter.

I know all this because I have been there. Unable to bring myself to accept Murgh's terms, I lost my head one night, seized a burning branch from the fire while the guard slept, and tried to escape through a small tunnel at the back of my cave. Murgh came after me and found me there, staring at the underground ruler of the island. She knew then, finally, that it was all right to take me to Julian.

Naturally he is insane. He no longer speaks, though he laughs sometimes in an angry, puzzled way as he works on his bugproof, computerless programs. The naked Stone Age people of the remote Northern village where he now lives regard him as the incarnation of Vala and bring him bananas and fresh fish every day. I have never found out whether his insanity was brought on by fear of the secret police or whether it was an innate condition crystallised by the girasol and the demons of Kuovala. If, then, else; who is to reason with madness?

Between the Walls

Peasant

The door was white once, but most of the paint has flaked off. The wood is grey and mouldering underneath. I am standing in a little closed alley between the backs of the houses, with a door at each end, just as if they wanted to defend themselves from the rest of the town. There is a pale green stalk over the lintel that turns this way and that, swollen with gnarls and knuckles, until it finally stops over the middle of the doorway and hangs its one white flower there. It is a rheumatism plant, the way it has all those joints. I have been looking at it ever since I arrived in this alley because that is the door he will come through.

I have already stayed two nights in this city and they cost me more than the whole of the rest of the journey, just for a patch of muddy floor by the doorway where people were stepping over me all night. My hand is in my purse. I can feel the farthings cool against my fingers, nuzzling them. I gave a boy three farthings for the news of the door and now I am counting the remaining coins to see whether I have enough for the journey back. My bread has gone; there are only a few dried crumbs in the bottom of the sack to remind me of home. The dried fish did not last either, or the onions.

In the alley there are just a couple of men kicking at stones and talking in their Roman language, which I do not understand, and also a young monk who does not seem to know where he is, reading his book and moving his lips the way they do. The Pope will pass this way, so the boy told me, but maybe he does not wish to go out at all. He may be staying in his palace, saying prayers in his golden chapel. It is true there are flowers hanging from the windows and the bells have been ringing since sunup, but how do I know? This city is full of cardinals, every one seventy times as powerful as the Baron. Father Arwin says there are six hundred and sixty-six of them and each has two handfuls of rings and every ring is worth enough to buy the Baron's palace and two hills of sheep to go with it. How do I know it is not one of them they are ringing for? There would be no point at all in going on my knees and weeping and begging an audience with a cardinal, however much his rings are worth. Father Arwin has explained it all to me: a cardinal is a duke of the Church, but only the Pope has the keys of St Peter. The Pope will be able to answer our questions.

He will ride through the door at the head of his procession. I think he will be a huge, powerful man with a crown on his head and carrying a sword in one hand and the keys of St Peter in the other. And there will be a glow coming from him like the paintings on the wall of the church. And he will see me kneeling humbly before him and fix me with round clear eyes like gold coins and say, Who is this fellow? He will say, *Fixibus, faxibus, horum harum abhominorum*, and the earth will shake, yes, the stones of the street will tremble under my knees, but I will get up and look him in those guinea eyes and say, May it please Your Lordship, in our own mud-and-butter tongue, since I am without Latin, and I shall hand him our petition.

May it please your Lordship, I am a humble man. I cannot read, nor write neither, but I come of a pious village and have been many nights on the road, sleeping among dust and small stones and insects such as I am not accustomed to, being by nature respectable. I bring you this petition, which may it please Your Lordship to read, being it is in sanctified Latin, written by our parish priest, Father Arwin. Also, although I cannot read it, may it please Your Lordship to know that I am apprised of the contents thereof, and so are all the men of the village, such as are of godly habits, and we do all consent to it.

WHEREAS it be generally agreed and understood by all that the generations of men do decline from great unto little and from virtue unto vice; and WHEREAS it be promised unto us in Holy Scripture that this unstable world shall not endure, but shall be utterly fractured, shattered and the powder thereof blown to the wind in the fullness of God's will; and WHEREAS it be known to the wise and the godly that certain signs and tokens will be displayed unto man in such fullness as a warning of the wrath to come; and WHEREAS this wrath is promised us in the one thousandth year of Our Lord, which is to say *Anno Domini*; we, the people of Harzwic wish humbly to advise and petition Your Lordship: ITEM, that a cockerel of unnatural size was lately seen in the waters near Harzwic coming out of the sea, having a great crest on his head and a great red beard and legs half a yard long; ITEM, that the number of stars falling from the sky in this year has been excessive and superabundant, and that many of the stars have fallen into the sea, which must infallibly cause them to be extinguished, and that there are no new ones to take their place; ITEM, that three wells to the north of Harzwic have been dried this summer by unusual heat, one being famed for the bowels and the ringworm, and small creatures do now live in it, having fins and legs; ITEM, that there be men in Harzwic who have books written in a strange language, not understood by our priest, Father Arwin, and we think these are of the devil; INASMUCH as we have presented these several ITEMS to Your Lordship, we, the godly people of Harzwic, do humbly invite Your

Lordship to consider and advise us whether the Day as is spoken of in Scripture be now nigh, especially as it is considered by the said Father Arwin that the next year may be that *Anno Domini* One Thousand of which the Scriptures do notify us, although he has not an almanac or other learned book to confirm this: and THEREFORE, if this Day be indeed approaching, we do beseech Your Lordship to pity us, and to plead for us with the Almighty, that we may be spared, as we are Godfearing people, and a list of our names be herewith enclosed. Witness my hand &c &c.

I stand here watching the door, feeling the farthings against my fingers, but I am not thinking about money any more. This is going to be the greatest thing that ever happened to me. I don't even care if the world does end now—it will have been worth it. Soon I am going to see the greatest Lordship of all, the nearest thing to God on earth, and I will speak to him in mud-and-butter and he will answer me in the *abhominorum* and he will reach out and take the parchment from my hand. Perhaps our fingers will touch and I will feel that power shoot through me like a golden arrow. Oh my stomach, my elbows! I don't care if I lose all my money and starve on the way home.

Why doesn't he come? It seems hours since I got here, and now the sun is right overhead. Does that monk feel the same as I do, I wonder? Perhaps he has a petition, too. What about the stone-kickers? What about the cardinal I saw just now going through the back door into one of the houses? Are they all waiting? I won't be able to stand it when that door opens. I shall fall on my face and not be able to get up.

When he comes through the door, I shall throw myself at his feet and say, May it please Your Lordship, the world is ending.

Cardinal

And so I sit in this room, which seems so dark because of the brightness outside, the dagger across my knees. I shall have to squeeze through this little window; it is a good thing I have kept my figure. The sun is high now. It slants across the roof opposite and is carved in two by the fine edge of my dagger. Why doesn't he arrive, anyway? The bells have been ringing for hours. I shall be glad when all this is over. These flowers they have hung everywhere make me sneeze. The room is full of dust. Every few minutes I am shaken by convulsions—it is like the last trump. People who do not suffer from it can have no idea. I pinch my nose hard to suppress the urge and fix my eyes on that flower over the doorway. That is the door to my destiny. When will it open?

Johannes Anglicus, he calls himself. When I met him, he was John of nowhere in particular; a skinny boy in an outsize cassock who did not dare look me in the eyes. Still, he was a pretty youth, and modest, knew his Bible, studious, could say Mass sweetly and as though he meant it—but knew nothing at all about the world. Leo was sick and couldn't last much longer; the College was divided between me and Anastasius Bibliotecharius, and I knew who the Emperor would support. For two months I was on an edge like the edge of this dagger, so fine I can hardly see it in the sunlight. I parried the messengers (I am still praying for a miracle—the Lord sees we are united in our love for the Holy Father). Some would have voted for me, perhaps enough, but I did not give them the chance. I had no wish to risk a schism, Bibliotecharius as Anti-Pope, Louis's soldiers marching on Rome, myself besieged in the Vatican, finally poisoned by some forgotten Frankish cook.

No, I am not a fool and I am not so greedy as my enemy. Greed is a great weakness in politicians. To achieve one's aims one must dedicate oneself to them with the devotion of an ascetic, one must stand on a spiritual pillar contemplating the mystery of the World from afar. For that reason I avoid wine and rich food, I live on bread, cheese and ale like a peasant, I have only the servants I have known since childhood. My one luxury is my books and I do not lose myself even in those. Yes, I think I am a kind of saint, not the ulcerated, dog-eared variety with which John sees fit to surround himself, but a saint for our times, a saint for the world. After all, I saw a vision, didn't I?

I must have fallen asleep reading in the orchard. I would not presume to say that I was awake at the time, for that would be excessive and inappropriate to a worldly saint. No, it was a dream, the medium by which God communicates with those of us who are not ready for the ulcers and the haloes—but the stealthy kind of dream, that does not announce itself as it would in the bedchamber, but is suddenly standing there among leaves and shadows and small red apples. Oh, it was a windfall of a dream. I know that I was sitting on my chair, the book on my lap and my eyes fixed on a point slightly beyond it, on my own bare calves and feet. And the dream stood in front of me unannounced. It did not even cough, but just waited for me to look up and see it. At first I did not look up: I stared into the tangle of grass at my feet as if to bury myself in its layers like a beetle. And then suddenly, without looking up or extricating my thoughts from the grass, I was staring it in the face and the face was that of Anastasius Bibliotecharius, that heavy, drooping face that looks as if he hasn't slept for a week, that solemn, stupid face. And he spoke: Why me? And then another man was standing beside him and I realised without surprise that it was myself; and I, too, said, Why me? And we began to multiply until the whole orchard was full of cardinals, all saying, Why me? In little twittering voices, like birds—it was all very charming. It was suggested, of course, by the red apples, as I realised the instant I awoke. But in the dream there was one figure that could not have been suggested by a red apple, since he was wearing his usual

61

outsize cassock. For once, he was not staring at the ground, but looking right at me. He is beautiful, you know, when he looks right at you. And he said nothing, but smiled, slowly, sweetly.

I did not change it much when reporting it to the College. I grant it was almost more of a fancy than a vision: the voice of God was not heard in it nor was there any manifestation of His presence or that of Our Lady and when it was all over I saw that the book had fallen from my knees and the sun was lower in the sky, thus indicating a common or garden dream. Nevertheless, it was a better vision than Anastasius could have had and the gist of it was truly ascetic. It had the surprisingness of divine inspiration, that unexpected rightness. Of course—an itinerant priest from nowhere in particular, a simple man, chosen of God, not (and this is the main thing) of the Emperor. For one blissful moment we were all united; we remembered what we represented in this world and—I do not exaggerate—God spoke through me. I declare that the day of his consecration was the happiest of my life. I really believed that God had used me as the instrument of His will. Johannes Anglicus, with the hand of God on his right shoulder and my own unworthy hand on his left, would rid the Church forever of the Emperor and his corruptions. A pure Church, a Church free from heresy, a Church that would rule the world and not be ruled by it. My intentions were honourable.

And for a while it seemed that I was right. The one or two danger signs that should have alerted me only confirmed my original judgement. First, the fact that John refused to remove his outsize cassock and don the robes and the mitre, either for his consecration or on any subsequent occasion. Next, the man he found begging at the gate and took into the palace and washed and dressed and fed on eggs and honey like one of his own pages. Then his long walks in the city alone, when he was said to stop at the houses of the poor and pray with them and give them money. All these things seemed good and holy to me! But then other things began to happen, strange things.

The papal court was suddenly full of alternative versions of John, men in outsize cassocks, men with country accents, who never looked one in the eye, who glowed with assumed righteousness, who cultivated sores and fleabites the way a gardener tends roses. They were John's saints. I pleaded with him: John, there cannot be so many saints in the world, or even if there are, not all in the same palace. Please, John, leave some for the humble people. And he said, We are all humble people, aren't we? And he laughed the way he does, and didn't look at me. Later, when Louis arrived in Bologna at the head of an army which seemed to be growing every day, trickling to him in dozens and fifties from every castle in the north of Italy, it was one of his saints John sent to talk to him. All right, Louis went home; I accept that. I don't understand it, but I accept it. Maybe anyone would go home rather than be confronted with more of those cassocks. I only know that it wasn't politics and that a palace full of fleas was too high a price to pay for peace. And that was not the worst of it. I could have tolerated the saints, even though they had entirely elbowed me out of John's confidence, even though the words *foreign policy* were never heard in his chambers any more, let alone *fiscal policy* or *administration*. But after the saints came a worse plague—the heretics!

There was that terrible morning when I entered the antechamber and found Epiphanius there, still with that smirk on his face, just as if he had never been away, still so clever: His Holiness has an open mind on doctrinal matters, Your Eminence—he wishes there to be a healthy atmosphere of debate and controversy in the palace. And all I could think of to say was, Oh yes, Epiphanius? And how was Wallachia? And I pleaded with John. I said, Father, you are not aware of the nuances of these matters. To fail to acknowledge the geographical reality of Paradise is halfway to making a metaphor of God Himself! We are not here to play games, Your Holiness! But he said, Personally I do not care very much where Paradise is. I felt sorry for him in those mountains.

And that was the beginning of the end, really. I used to trip over them in hallways and push past them on the stairs, little knots of men discussing the immanence of the divine and the circularity of time, the existence of alternative universes, the numbers, ranks and powers of angels and demons. When they saw me they would fall silent suddenly and one or two of them would giggle. Oh, there is something deeply indecorous about a wizened scholar of sixty giggling. And how did it make me feel? Like a feeble schoolmaster, a schoolmaster robbed of my cane. And I said to myself, this must stop. The Church is no longer the Church. We are an ark of unclean beasts.

So. He will come though that door in the wall on his horse and the procession will be forced to ride in one at a time because of the narrowness of the street. Eulalius will be second or third in the file (with a Pope as vague as John on matters of precedence, this will have been easy for him to arrange). He will cause his horse to shy at the door, holding up the others, and my men will close the door, trapping John in the alley. Of course, there will be the guards who ride in front of him, but they will be helpless in the confined space. My men will drop from the windows and overhanging roofs of the neighbouring houses. The guards will be overpowered in moments. I will take John myself, with my ancestor's knife with the carved wooden handle. It will not be a pleasant duty, but it is mine alone. I started this and only I can finish it.

When he comes through the door, I shall bury my dagger in his saintly heart.

Monk

I stand in this alleyway with a peasant and one or two military-looking oafs kicking stones. We are the riffraff, who do not line the streets and cheer like everyone else, but skulk between narrow walls as if in ambush. Never mind. If I can only see him, I shall be happy.

I still say that: if I can only see him! How ridiculous of me —that is what I still think. That was what I thought when I was so much younger, last year, when I heard of the Pope who was making so many changes, the Pope who believed in debate. I thought I must see him and tell him my idea. There was nobody else worthy to listen to it. No one in the monastery understood me. I even applied to the Archbishop, the old fool. They do not know what it is to have a genius among them. That was what I thought because I was so much younger than I am now, and I fled from the monastery and made my way to Rome, sleeping by day and travelling by night like an outlaw, eating leaves and wild berries, never knowing which were good and which poisonous, trusting to the Lord to protect me. In those days, when I was younger, an idea was bread, wine and fire to me. I needed nothing else. I can hardly remember what the idea was, now. It had to do with Ephesians, I know that much. I realise now I was in love with myself and that was why I was so sure that my perceptions were brilliant and unique.

I barged past the guards at the door (I must see him—it is about Ephesians. Yes, of course he will understand. He is the Pope), not knowing, then, how easy it was to get an audience. The guards had given up looking at people. They could no longer tell which sort was acceptable and which was not. Once inside, I was lost. I remember a huge panelled hall with torches burning on the walls, even though it was daylight, where disreputable-looking men sat about on the rushes examining their toenails. (I must look like that, I thought.) When I asked them where the Pope was, no one knew. Some of them did not even realise they were in the Vatican; others were buried in books, either reading or writing them, and did not care where they were. I found similar men in corridors, asleep on the floor or squatting with their backs to the walls gazing into eternity.

I don't know how long I wandered in the palace, eating nothing, lying on the floor when sleep caught up with me, surprised when passing a window to notice that it was day again, or night. And then, at one special window, I looked out and saw the courtyard, the nutmeg tree, the fountain, the youth leaning over the edge watching the fish. Why, I thought, he is only a boy. He is no older than I am. But I knew right away that it was him.

Sir, I said, Your Holiness, I must speak with you. It is a theological matter. And he looked up and said, Oh yes? And I was vaguely disappointed. I felt I had disappointed *him*, as if there were other matters he would rather talk about than theology. And he said, Come down here, but I didn't know the way, so he met me on the stairs, and we talked in the courtyard until the sun set. (Have you eaten? No, I see you haven't. You must be half dead. You came all this way to tell me this. It amazes me the sacrifices people make to tell me things, as if it was important. Never mind—come inside and I will get you something to eat.) And later, when I was slightly drunk and we were talking in front of a huge fire somewhere with logs crashing down, and the crackling in my ears deafened me, he said, You still don't understand, do you? Priests are so stupid. All men are stupid, but especially priests. Look—and he put his hand on my shoulder—let me show you.

Femina est! In the firelight I discovered the source of sin, the genesis of mortality! I touched her small breasts, I burned my fingers on the flame of her nipples and the ember between her legs. What oil can soothe those burns? Afterwards she lay on the ground, her cropped boy's head nestling in the rushes, her scrawny white body flickering in sleep and I gazed at her, sick and terrified.

When she comes through the door I shall throw myself at her horse's feet and cry, Bless me, Mother, for I have sinned!

Pope

Even now, as I ride at the head of this procession, I would like to throw myself to the ground in front of the cheering people and say, Forgive me, good people—I am not as you suppose. I am only a humble woman who never wished to do wrong. It was only priests who made me this way. If it were not for priests I would be happy and not have committed sin. Ah! I am punished. And anyway, I could have had Simon or Roger or Ranulph, and now I would be in a hut sweeping the floor or boiling beetroot and would want for nothing else, only I was tempted by Eustace because he was so good and sweet and did not fight with sticks like the rest of them. It was Eustace who taught me my *Kyrie* and my *Credo in Unum Deum*, who showed me *caritas* and I looked at his brown eyes and thought only of *eros*. Oh, and for him I read my Bible, such as a woman should not know how to read, but only because I was clever and in love. I did not know it would come to harm. And one afternoon he had me among the lettuces when the boys were out in the fields and there was blood on the leaves, and he said, It is natural—it will sink into the soil and nourish them. But then next day he had gone, gone in a hurry no one knew where, without his cassock or breviary, and I took them to Rome. Ah! (The pains are getting closer.) I went to Rome because that was where a priest should go if anywhere, because it is where God lives, and I went after him because I was married to a priest, as I thought then, and I should be with my husband. And I stood on street corners wearing his cassock and preached to the people because it was all I could do to get a little alms for bread. And I hoped thereby to make myself known so he would come to see me. Oh, it hurts, it hurts!

And I was known, but to the wrong person, for it was not Eustace who came to hear but a superannuated Eustace, a Eustace *in excelso*, surpassing him in age and holiness and wickedness. It was my weakness that made me say Johannes instead of Johanna, not impertinence. I never wished to be other than I am. I do not wish it even now, even though it hurts so much. I did not mean to be a priest and I still do not understand how I became the Pope. I thought it was all a dream for weeks and when I no longer hoped to awaken all I could think was if Eustace could see me now, if Eustace could live in the palace and be the Pope's husband all might yet be well. Oh, you are a mad woman, Joan. So I went out in the streets and I asked the people if they knew anyone who was a priest, or who might once have been a priest but had lost his cassock and his breviary, but the men they showed me were never the right ones. But these people stuck to me like sheep's wool on a hedge. They clung to me as if I was a saint or a doctor, until the palace was not my own any more and I could not move for paupers and lepers. Every day they would stare at me with their empty eyes and I would see Eustace as he might have become, a Eustace sick and suffering because of me. He has been punished too, I thought—we must save each other.

And then one day by the fountain, I looked up and for a moment I thought it was him—it was his own brown eyes. And in the courtyard until the sun went down I held him with learned talk, the way I had learned from Eustace, and later by the fire I held him with my arms and with my ankles. And he must have been another Eustace, because when I woke with my face hot from the flames and my *pudendum* aching, when I pulled the rushes from my hair, he was gone again. And now, ah, I am punished for my presumption.

I do not know why everywhere I go it becomes a procession. I should just skulk off into a corner and give birth like a she-animal. I do not want to be followed. Oh, the waters are breaking. It is a new deluge—they must all see it running off the robes and dripping on the pavement. But no one sees anything in a crowd like this. There is an alley ahead. If I could shut them out somehow, I could be alone to bring it into the world.

Not it, him. I know it will be a boy. I shall hide away in the alley and give birth to a boy, and his name shall be Eustace. I will teach him his Latin, for he will have no father to do it for him, and he will have brown eyes, and when he is old enough he will be a priest. But not the Pope. He will not be that, because it is too complicated, even for a man. Ah! I see the door ahead. If I can just make it as far as the door.

Green Winter

It is dark when the guards come to wake me. For a moment I imagine that I am back home and that some catastrophe has taken place, a fire, perhaps, or a burglary, but then I remember and swear at them. Yuri grins and says, 'Come with us. The Director has visitors.'

Outside, the stars have already faded and the only light comes from a few scraps of muddy snow. The white winter is over and the green winter is beginning; it has been thawing for a week now and I tread carefully to avoid the deep, slushy puddles that are scattered everywhere, colder than snow itself. I must still be half-asleep, because a line of English poetry suddenly appears in my head:

Woken in the pre-dawn by my guards…

Where does it come from? Have I read it somewhere?

The Director smiles, just like Yuri, and says, 'Come in, come in, please take a seat. A cold morning for the time of year, isn't it?'

'It isn't morning,' I tell him sullenly.

It is warm in the office. There is a charcoal stove, a big one, and an electric light, though without a shade. To make it look more like an office and less like a caretaker's hut, there is a desk with a typewriter on it and one of those wire intrays you see in Moscow offices. I am not deceived, however. Tigran Vartanovitch is not in favour. Zhelatsk is not one of the more modern camps—it is the true end of the world, *ultima Thule*. The Director must have said the wrong thing at a cocktail party or perhaps he was at the wrong cocktail party altogether.

I am given a cup of coffee, which scalds my palate and tastes, enigmatically, of paraffin, but for which I am grateful. The Director introduces me to his visitors, a tall, athletic

70

bald man from Budapest, Dr Koshka, and a small, crumpled bald man from Moscow, Dr Simagin. Koshka, the Hungarian, is an eminent parapsychologist, and Simagin, a representative of the Supreme Committee for the Advancement of Soviet Science—in other words, I assume, some sort of policeman, even if an inductive rather than a deductive one. They ask me a number of questions about what they refer to as my 'powers'.

'I have no powers,' I tell them impatiently.

I have no powers. When it comes to clairvoyance, I am just as likely to be spectacularly wrong as spectacularly right. If I had powers, after all, I would be making a fortune in black market beef carcasses or selling secrets to the Americans instead of languishing in this desolate place, the period of cosmography, the blank zone on the map. Unfortunately I cannot control the visions that come to me when I lie in my hut at night, any more than I can control the cold or the darkness. Knowledge is only power if it is knowledge that somebody wants and mine is not. Sometimes I wonder if even I want it.

Recently, my visions have been of a man of about forty, handsome in a craggy way, an Englishman, a poet. Sometimes I see him in bed with a blonde, frail woman, the wife of his publisher. (He addresses her as Ro, a curious syllable that might be the Greek letter or the English word for fish eggs.) They argue frequently about literary awards, about travel grants he might get to go to Iceland or America, about a man called Simpkins of whom the poet is jealous. At other times I see him in village halls, or in cold, varnish-scented seminar rooms, reading impassioned descriptions of his childhood to sparse audiences of uncomfortable and adoring females. Sometimes again he is doing something mundane, like going to the lavatory or buying razor blades, but I see him with such vividness that I *am* the poet, I smell the soap or see the foreign money in the till. I am not myself. It is my only distinction that I am not always myself.

It is typical of my unevenness that, although the visitors are obviously interested in my spiritual, not my family life, my famous intuition at once leads me to believe that something has happened to Yelyena. Either she has received permission to go into exile—I mean the real kind, external exile—or she has been arrested, or she is dead. Dead—I am sure it is the latter. I do not know whether a political death or whether she has just died, but the voice has spoken.

On the contrary, Simagin tells me I am to be asked to take part in an experiment in the interests of the health and happiness of the Soviet people. For me, it will mean a transfer to Moscow, visits from Yelyena and the children, an end to the hard labour that is ruining my health. Dr Koshka, who is the Professor of Parapsychology at Moscow State Technical College, has assembled more than a hundred gifted psychics for the experiment, which involves, Simagin implies, our national security. Of course, what I learn in this hut is to go no further.

Simagin now becomes rhetorical and refers to great leaps being made in the name of Soviet science by beings that he does not define. Then Koshka takes over and asks for the light to be extinguished so that he can show a film. The Director, excitingly, dismisses the guards, and a white, flickering square, a *Thule*, is projected on the wall as Koshka struggles with the film. A luminous countdown flashes past: 10-9-8-7-6-5-4-3-2-1. The film begins.

> Scene One. Koshka, three or four years younger, walks down a Moscow street with a large red question mark poised over his head.
>
> VOICEOVER: Have you ever wished you could do something with the unused parts of the brain? Close-up of puzzled frown behind Koshka's hornrimmed spectacles. Cut to:

Scene Two. Very dingy studio set intended to represent a laboratory. Two Soviet scientists, identified as such by white coats and Order of Lenin round neck, are pouring frothing liquid into test-tubes.

VOICEOVER: Soviet scientists have been labouring night and day to liberate the full power of the brain for the sake of science, socialism and the advancement of humanity.

Cut to:

Scene Three. Old black-and-white film of Egyptian desert, clearly from pirated travelogue.

VOICEOVER: This is a pyramid.

'What was that about pyramids?' I ask, as someone behind me scrabbles to find the light switch.

The bulb explodes into brightness above my head, and the Director, ignoring my question, says, 'I hope you found that interesting.'

'But it's only just started.'

'What do you mean?' the Director demands, but Koshka squats in front of my chair and peers curiously into my eyes.

'What was the last scene you remember?' he asks.

The question is so simple that I have a horrible feeling there must be a catch in it, but I reply anyway. 'The pyramids.'

'You've been asleep!' the Director says indignantly.

'Is that so?' Koshka asks.

'No. Yes. No, not asleep.'

'Not asleep? Absent, perhaps?'

'Yes,' I reply, 'absent.'

After all it is not easy to live in a mosaic. If Koshka had not squatted in front of my chair and searched my eyes as he did, I would not know myself why I missed the film. It is like clambering out of a dream and then, when you finally emerge, being unable to remember whether you had the dream last night, or the night before or whether it was a dream at all. There are only the little coloured stones to be fitted in somewhere.

For most of the film, I now realise, I was in England with the poet, who was in bed with a woman—his own wife, this time, rather than someone else's. Her name is Tess, and she differs from his other monosyllabic lover in almost every respect. Where Ro is blonde, Tess is dark. Where Ro has bony shoulders, Tess, from what I have been able to see of her above the duvet, is rather buxom. But her post-coital temper is just as fierce as Ro's. (It is a disappointment to me that I always seem to arrive in my other existence just after the fun has stopped and end up doing the agonising instead of the ecstasising.) Tess was reproaching me for my infidelity, which she claimed was very immature. I defended myself on the grounds that Ro is better placed than almost anybody in England to advance my career. In bed, she is a *femme de lettres* in her own right. She has had sex with all sixteen members, male and female, of the Firm, the group of poets who run the literary scene from their country houses in Oxfordshire and Gloucestershire, and thus has the power to cause domestic disharmony on a Parnassian scale. Poets are nothing if not domestic animals.

My English self, of course, is no exception to this rule, but he is not afraid that Tess will leave him. She is proud of his status as the leading poet of his generation and the likely next member of the Firm. The blood of Shakespeare and Milton flows in his veins, as she sees it, and indeed she is probably right. In any case, the poet talked so convincingly about his power over Ro and Ro's power over the English literary world that she finally fell asleep with a glow of enthusiasm suffusing her as far down as the sternum. The poet, however—or was it me by this time?—was not so sure. But then poets never are.

The photograph which Koshka hands me is of a grey-haired man smiling in an eminent way as if discreetly attempting to show off his gold fillings.

'Do you know this man?' Koshka asks. I shake my head.

'You are sure?'

'Yes.'

'You would not like to guess his name? His nationality? Anything about him?'

'No.'

Koshka seems disappointed. He runs his hand over his scalp and begins to pace up and down. 'I am sorry you missed my film,' he says eventually. 'I would show it again, but it will be dawn soon and the curtains here would probably not be adequate to keep out the light. Never mind. Let me tell you something about myself.'

He continues walking very rapidly, more like a man on a military exercise than one struggling with a train of thought. He explains that the film showed how he, Koshka, had had a mysterious vision of the shooting of a certain president in a foreign country and how the president was, in fact, assassinated several months later. How Koshka always remembered afterwards exactly where he was when he heard the news (in Dnyepopetrovsk railway station, returning from a conference). How he took the next train to Moscow instead of going home, and how he was, after the necessary checks had been made, offered the Chair of Parapsychology, the first of its kind in the history of Soviet further education. How he conducted experiments in levitation, teleportation, telepathy and clairvoyance. Finally, the film showed his major finding, that a large number of gifted individuals concentrating their psychic forces on a single target could produce extraordinary effects, both physical and psychological.

Koshka stops his pacing and directs my attention to the photograph again. 'Suppose such a man were the target,' he says.

'Who is he?'

'Suppose he were the ambassador of a foreign power hostile to the Soviet Union.'

'Yes?'

'Suppose, then, that more than a hundred of the most gifted psychics in the country were gathered together in one place—say, Moscow State Technical College, for the sake of argument—and they knew a great deal about the man. They might have done some research, and found out that he had a mistress in Wisconsin (or wherever he came from) to whom he still wrote occasionally; that as a boy he was sickly and suffered from rheumatic fever; that he once dreamed of being a professional basketball player, but was not tall enough; that his mother was dying of Parkinson's disease; that the food he missed most in his present posting was corned beef. You understand the kind of information I mean?'

'I think so.'

'The kind it takes to know a man thoroughly. Suppose these gifted individuals knew such a man in this way, and that they used their knowledge against him. Suppose they concentrated on him for an hour a day, trying to influence him, to change his behaviour. What do you think would happen?'

'I don't know.'

'Might he make a mistake? Perhaps send a letter to his government full of erroneous information?'

'I don't know.'

'Alternatively, might he walk into the nearest police station and ask for political asylum?'

'I don't know.'

'Finally, might he not fall unexpectedly ill? Have a stroke or suffer from hallucinations?'

'I don't know. How do you expect me to know?'

'I don't expect it,' Koshka replies smiling. 'We don't know, either.'

A study. I know it is a study although I have never been in one before. Through a small window opposite the door, I can see some typical English scenery of a green variety, downland or heath or moorland—I am not familiar with the technical vocabulary. There is a single bed, suitable for throwing oneself on when worn out by the act of creation, and also a desk, brilliant and significant in the disc of light thrown by an anglepoise lamp (even though it is daylight beyond the window). The walls are heavy with books. A man of about forty, handsome in a craggy way, is sitting at the desk writing a poem:

Woken in the pre-dawn by my guards…

It is to be a political poem, a protest against the injustice of the Soviet system. It will be thick with authentic detail: black bread, small green fish eaten whole, tattered cloths bound round the feet instead of shoes. It will be tense with a reticent British courage and it will win a major poetry competition because of its realism and political awareness:

…I ask nothing
but time to dream of my childhood,
the odour of crushed blackberries,
sausage and soap and forgotten love affairs.
But there is not very much time. Dawn is breaking.

Dawn is breaking as I explain to Dr Koshka and Dr Simagin that I am obliged to refuse their offer. The reason I give is not political or even moral. I explain that I am an individualist and do not think I could work well with other psychics, that the substance inside me doesn't appear to mix. Also that, as I remarked earlier, my faculties are passive ones and I have never influenced anybody to do anything in my life. It may be so, of course. The thought crosses my mind that I may perhaps have influenced an English poet whose name I still do not know to write a poem about me that would never otherwise have been written. An alternative and more uncomfortable thought is that I may, in fact, have no existence outside his poem and that this may explain my refusal to act in my own best interests, a common failing of fictional characters.

Koshka seems neither angry nor disappointed. He has, after all, more than a hundred psychics for his experiment. The guards are summoned again to take me to breakfast. As we leave the hut, a small remote sun is shining and the icy green of the surrounding fields looks suddenly foreign.

Sleevenotes

Lost Lunches, the Very Best of Colin Crab and the Ptomaines

Remember when a sleeve was a sleeve? In the antediluvian days of 12-inch vinyl long players, of *albums* no less, the packaging was part of the package, right? It's a personal theory of mine that the record sleeve was the rock video of its day, purveying the image, face, presence of the artist in much the same way that the aforementioned televisual masquerade was to do for a CD generation accustomed to getting its musical kicks out of a plastic jewel case with a four-inch-square snap on the cover. A sleeve was an experience, from the wet-dream-fuelling glam-shlock nudity of the Roxy Music covers to the wallpaper-paste minimalism of the Clash and the Pistols, from the multi-hued lava lamp gloop that swirled over offerings from Yes and King Crimson to the oh-so-knowing Kodachrome surrealism pioneered by Hipgnosis. (Remember them?)

And now? The bozos from Editions Zippo have ordained that I write a so-called sleevenote (actually a prim little booklet that goes *inside* the box) for the new greatest hits compilation from a geezer who looms not unlarge in my own particular past. Come to think of it, those Editions Zippo bozos loom not unlarge in my past, too. Remember *Scratch 'n' Sniff*, guys? Time was, when you were the ones writing 500-word sleevenotes to eke out the meagre wages you garnered for making the tea and sweeping up the roaches from the office floor or whatever you did, while I was the chief feature-writer and all-round coolest dude in the territory.

This reviewer's first encounter with Crab and his cohorts took place at the Empire Tombola, Perivale at the fag-end of '76. Picture the scene. So early is it in the New Wave era that at least half the punters are wearing flares. Spiked coiffures are in evidence, but so too are the standard shoulder-length split ends. The music over the PA is Eddie and the Hot Rods, then thought of by many of the cognoscenti as the cutting edge of 70s sounds. And I'm standing at the back of the hall in my shades and biker jacket, dodging the flying beercans and trying not to feel old. I've been sent by my long-suffering editor to cover a gig by the Rolling Donuts, a shortlived combo out of North Acton. Fact is, I ought to be at home here, because Perivale is practically my backyard, raised as I was in the boondocks of Ealing Common. Fact is, I'm not; it took a major arm twisting episode on the part of said editor to induce me to put my schnozzle round the door, to hear a band I'd never heard of playing in a venue known to be the weeknight haunt of cardigan-clad grannies. Check it out, said the editor. So here I was, cowering under the swoosh of low-flying Carlsbergs, my toes crushed by pogoing teens, checking out the Donuts. And boy did they suck. The support band, tho', had a certain... Hang on a minute, while I count the words. Start again.

Lost Lunches, the Very Best of Colin Crab and the Ptomaines

Remember when a sleeve was a sleeve? If you sometimes feel regret for the era of 12-inch vinyl longplayers, of fold-out album covers and funny little inserts with the lyrics printed on them (the best titles used to be mostly in brackets, right? And the best lyrics diverged mysteriously from what the vocalist actually sang), the enclosed will take you right back to those glory days of coffee-stained cardboard. Not that Colin Crab and the Ptomaines were ever about nostalgia. Back in '76 when Perivale was the fulcrum of London's burgeoning punkopolis, seemed like any kid with a stripy tie hanging round his neck could grab a mike and cough out his adolescent spleen all over the greying patriarchs of Tin Pan Alley and Desolation Row. *In absentia*, natch—the ilk of Jagger, Townsend and Clapton wouldn't have been seen dead at Perivale's Empire Tombola club on a Saturday night, knowing as they did that being seen dead there was the only available option. For the seen-it-all music hacks of that era, among whom I number myself and my compadres at *Scratch 'n' Sniff* magazine (some of them, by a curious coincidence, currently administering Crab's back-catalogue in the deep-pile offices of Editions Zippo), this *lèse-majesté* was refreshing. In '76, just about everybody knew that a revolution was coming, and that just-about-everybody includes not only 18-year-olds like Colin Crab, the erstwhile Ron Feathergill, but also battle-weary 29-year-old scribblers like myself, author of so many paeans to rock operas and concept albums that I was just about all paeaned out.

Looming out of the murk of smoke and sputum on that vinyl-dark November night, the Ptomaines seemed little better than your average teenage no-hopers, fuelled by spite and acne. The bass-player wore pyjamas—a standard mode of dress, then, for would-be punks who couldn't find any drainpipes in their local Oxfam shop. The drummer had stepped straight out of some time-warp saloon bar, still in his rugby shirt and Beatle haircut, and was thudding away as if engaged in some weird callisthenics. The guitarist was a scrawny-moustached runt whose axe was always on the verge of getting away from him, dragging him round the stage like an out-of-control lawnmower. But vocalist Crab was the undoubted star. A tall man, he seemed to grow when he sang, till by the end of the last number he was about seven foot two. Then there were the limbs. While others limit themselves to four, max, he sported at least eight and frequently more as he whirled them around, smashing lights, mikes and kit—seldom has the rationale of a stage moniker been more apparent. He had a whooping way of singing, an unexpectedly contralto sound from such a scary-looking individual. Curlews aren't heard too often in NW17 and I can't claim to be familiar with their call, but on the few nights I've lain awake brooding on ornithology, that is the

noise I've attributed to them in my mind. As for the lyrics...
That's 500.

Lost Lunches, the Very Best of Colin Crab and the Ptomaines

In '76, when many authorities were shrugging off bands like
the Damned, the Clash and the Pistols as a phase, I and my
colleagues at the late lamented *Scratch 'n' Sniff* magazine had
had them pegged as the next big thing for so long that the
more forward-thinking among us were already starting to
think of them as the last big thing. Seemed to us that they
were in danger of forgetting their roots and selling out. Any
moment now they would be releasing albums, appearing on
Top of the Pops, playing the Albert Hall. And so we started
our search for the acts that would replace them in the
popular imagination when everyone had heard of them.

My first encounter with Colin Crab and the Ptomaines,
whose raucous riffs 'n' chops, heard to advantage on this
compilation, eminently qualified them for the role, took
place in the unlikely-sounding setting of the Empire
Tombola, Perivale. My first encounter with Crab himself was
even more unlikely. After the gig, I staggered to the toilet,
where, finding my path to the urinal barred by a giggle of
safety-pinned girlfriends drinking beer from the can and
admiring the rear aspect of their *beaux*, I entered one of the
cubicles. From the other side of the partition came the
rhythmic grunt-squeal of a couple who hadn't been able to
wait till they got home, 6/8 time. I was standing there
minding my own business when the door was pushed
forcibly into my back. Turning—carefully—I recognised the
lead singer of the evening's support band. What was their
name again? Not at all fazed by the sight of my unplugged
equipment, Crab proceeded to offer me a drag on the joint
he had (with charming caution) come in to smoke. We
finished that spliff, and a second and the then, and indeed

perennially, homeless vocalist accepted my invitation to spend the night at my gaff.

Crab had a clipped, almost military way of speaking. 'Name's Ron,' he said when I introduced him to my girlfriend (the Colin Crab handle was strictly for showbiz purposes). Caroline was not exactly pleased to welcome a stoned youth into her home at midnight, but Ron's reticent manners soothed her so effectually that she made up a bed for him on the sofa—'with pillows and everything,' as he put it. He was greatly taken with our few items of furniture, the bentwood-style Habitat rocking chair on which he propelled himself to and fro with deep concentration for almost half an hour, the giant beanbag he couldn't stop punching and squeezing, delighted at the rattle it made. 'Nice house,' he kept saying (it was always a house to him, never a flat). He can't have been comfortable on our strictly two-seater sofa; it took a sustained effort from all three of us to arrange his semi-independent limbs under the blankets, and by the end of it we were all laughing so hard we didn't feel like sleeping anyway. Shit.

Lost Lunches, the Very Best of Colin Crab and the Ptomaines

If the juggernaut of the nostalgia industry has now rolled as far as the late 1970s, that seems just. Hasn't rock 'n' roll always been about destroying the past, and hasn't it always had to face, over and over, the fact that it, in its turn, has become the past it wanted to destroy?

These thoughts are prompted by the re-emergence of Colin Crab and his estimable band the Ptomaines in this shitkicking compilation, *Lost Lunches*, sadly not available in vinyl with its sensuous tactile qualities and potential for external sleevenotes. To hear Crab wailing his fuckyou anthems over the Ptomaines' static-frazzled thrash is to be transported to another time, another place.

For the present writer, the place in question is my own living room, where Colin Crab, aka Ron Feathergill, resided for a short period, during which I taught him blues harp. The band only knew three chords, but seldom bothered with more than one of them in any given song. So the harp offered an extra dimension of raw plangency to the most basic of formulas. 'Had one of these when I was a kid,' Ron said. 'From Woolies.' He seemed interested for a while. I showed him how to bend the notes, but when he proved unable to emulate the feat, he grew bored, threw the instrument to the floor and jumped up and down on it, listlessly. 'Sounds like a strangled cat,' he said.

'That's how the blues is,' I told him.

'You could just strangle a cat,' he replied. 'It'd be easier.'

It was a shock to be confronted with someone who really didn't give a shit as opposed to acting like he didn't give a shit within certain prescribed limits. If Ron had asked me for hair gel, I would have been able to provide him with some. Such was the home-made ethos of punk, tho', that it would never have occurred to Ron to use a bought cosmetic on his follicles. His solution was to go to the fridge and dig out a fistful of butter. It was days before we identified the source of the rancid grease smeared over our soft furnishings.

Ron never slept at night. This was no problem for me, used to a life of late gigs and elastic deadlines. To Caroline, on the other hand, who had to get up at seven-thirty to go to work, his habit of kicking a tennis-ball round the living-room in the small hours, or walking into our bedroom saying he was bored, was infuriating. So too was the way he kept open house for his friends. If I got up in the night I'd usually find a small group playing Monopoly on the carpet. Bass-player Eugene Winceyette would be there, sporting the pyjamas that made him look more at home than I did shivering in my briefs. There was also a fat tarot-reading woman who turned out to be Ron's mother. Little did I know then what the cards... Fuck this job.

Lost Lunches, the Very Best of Colin Crab and the Ptomaines

In the late 70s, as the New Wave broke over the rock world, geezers like Colin Crab arose, intent on overthrowing everything that had gone before. And other, slightly older, geezers like, arguably, the present reviewer, wrote articles about how cool they were, whatever secret reservations we may have had about their musical abilities and the whole nihilistic project they represented. Y'see, deep down, some of us couldn't help feeling that, despite everything we could do by way of radical hairdressing and new trousers and, uh, earrings, we were becoming the past ourselves, and that maybe the time had come to stand up and be—I was going to say *counted*, but possibly *dated* would be nearer the mark.

'That's what I wanna get across,' I said. I was slowly sinking into the carpet of an office the size and temperature of an imperial mausoleum. Except that the Emperor was still alive, seated on a pile of grey plastic cushions behind a plastic mahogany desk with a plastic aspidistra on it. The air was rich with the scent of a dozen different species of plastic, some of them previously unknown in the West. I wanted to sit down, but there were no chairs as such in the room, only a few dangerous-looking plastic assemblies obviously intended as satirical *hommages* to chairs, some of them with backs and seats but no legs, some with seats and legs but no backs, some with legs but no seats or backs.

I had been dragged into the enemy's citadel to be told in no uncertain terms that my bollocks were on the line. The bozo confronting me was none other than my own former *protégé* Ali Wilco, now commissioning editor for textual packaging. He was dressed in a camouflage jumpsuit, paratrooper style, and swiveling a toothpick from one side of his mouth to the other with his tongue.

'You could've come in any time you wanted, y'know, Jeff. It must be tough out there.' He gave a vague shake of his carefully distressed locks in the direction of the window. Note *could've* come in, meaning *can't come in any more*.

'That's the street, Ali. You may remember a lot of us used to believe in it.'

'Yeah, mate, but we didn't wanna live there, did we? The important thing was the word on it, as far as I remember. You can still hear that up here, in comfort.'

I tried to shuffle my feet, but they were too far in.

'Look, all I want is 500 words on Colin Crab and the Ptomaines. You can knock that off in an afternoon. What's so difficult? They weren't even any good.' He picked up my latest typescript, glanced at it, dropped it again. 'Get yourself a computer. Who types, these days?'

'I'm trying, Ali. Out of practice, that's all.'

'C'mon, Jeff, you can do this shit with your eyes shut. Visceral, seminal, quintessential etc, etc. You taught me.'

'Thing is, Ali, there's a lot of history there.'

Lost Lunches, the Very Best of Colin Crab and the Ptomaines

It's easy at this distance to characterise the New Wave era as a time of excess. In fact, by '76 when punk had long been making inroads into the noodles of those of us who considered ourselves wired in to the music scene, excess seemed to have peaked. What was notable about the eponymous hero of the present offering was his innocence. The joint he smoked with this writer in the john at the Empire Tombola, Perivale, was, he later confided, his first ever. And while he came on like a cynical urban Lothario in his lyrics, he was still so inexperienced with women that the presence of my girlfriend Caroline in the same flat filled him with awe. I've seen him seize one of her bras from the tumble-dryer and play with it for hours, rubbing his cheek against the cups and gnawing at the flimsy straps.

(Fortunately, she was absent at the time.) And tho' I never actually caught him trying to peek through the keyhole while Caroline was in the bath, he used to knock at the door and ask to come and get a comb or a razor he'd left therein. After his first couple of nights as our guest, we figured that his habit of wandering into our bedroom in the small hours was not just down to boredom, as he claimed, and took to pushing the wardrobe in front of the door, an arrangement which initially caused outbursts of petulant hammering on his part, but which he later came to accept.

Ron's mum, Violet, was increasingly a fixture in our gaff, sitting on the sofa which served as Ron's bed with her tarot cards spread out on the coffee table, offering to read the fortune of anyone who happened to be passing. Inevitably, the time came when I consulted her myself. The question I asked the cards concerned Ron's continuing presence in the flat. In my head—Violet told me it was important not to say it out loud. Unlike other tarot mavens of my acquaintance (they occasionally showed up at the *Scratch 'n' Sniff* offices in the mystical days of the early 70s) she didn't just deal the pack from the top, but sorted through it carefully, studying the front of each card, then my face, then the card again, a process that reminded me of having my photograph taken, tho' it was more like being painted, I guess. Like all the other mavens, however, she told me Death didn't actually mean Death. (It appears without fail whenever I get the cards read, but it does that for everyone, right?) At the centre of the spread was the King of Cups reversed, which she said represented a person who had been receiving my hospitality, and directly underneath was the Ten of Swords. 'Looks bad, dear,' she said. 'Bit of a dustup with someone. And the answer to your question is, not for a while. He's got a few things to get sorted first.'

For all the sociopolitical ramifications of the New Wave, an album such as the present one stands or falls by the excellence or otherwise of the songs. If Colin Crab and the Ptomaines have survived long enough to spawn a *Very Best Of* compilation, the music must have lasting qualities. For that staying-power, the author of this note must take a degree of responsibility. *Caroline*, for example, the heroine of Crab's bittersweet lovesong (is that *bath* or *barf* he rhymes with *laugh*?) was my girlfriend of the time, the object of his shy admiration until he began his relationship with the lady he celebrates / excoriates in *Lancia*—note that I said lady, not car, which should clear up a common misinterpretation.

Way I recall it, I rose at past noon that day, having stayed late at a gig and ensuing festivity the night before. Caroline was at work, and the flat was silent. As it turned out, Ron had expelled all his usual guests (including his mother, Violet, the only woman I have ever met who cheated at tarot), and was sitting on the sofa with a girl who looked about twelve years old, dressed in the odd mixture of *up-yours* and *come-hither* that punkettes affected—massive purple ribbon on top of the head, studded leather jacket, razor-blade dangling from one ear, scrawny white flesh protruding through cunningly placed rips in the T-shirt. There was a good six inches of neutral cushion between them, and they were both staring straight ahead.

'Who the fuck's this?' the girl said.

'Geezer that lives here,' Ron replied, adding, in roughly my direction, 'You wanna go out an' buy some garlic or something?' Ron was a frugal eater, preferring plain boiled rice to anything else, but under Caroline's influence had taken to flavouring it with raw garlic.

'We've got garlic.'

'Well, go an' get something else then.'

They were not so modest subsequently. After that first day, they would get it on in full view of everyone present, tho' fully clothed as was the fashion at the time (it was what all those zippers were for). Caroline would make an excuse and leave the room at such moments, while the rest of us just carried on with whatever we were doing. Lancia was small and squeaky, particularly during orgasm. I asked Ron once what he saw in her. 'She's all fluffy,' he said.

Ron's new love was a constant irritation to Caroline, surreptitiously borrowing her sanitary towels and contraceptive pills. 'They can both fuck off,' she would whisper at night as we lay barricaded in our bedroom. 'They can get out of my fucking flat. I'm not having him screwing his bint on my sofa.' She didn't know how soon she was to get her wish. Crab and the band had another gig booked at the Empire Tombola, this time topping the bill, and I had arranged for a senior honcho from Bicycle Records to check it out. The big time was waiting.

Lost Lunches, the Very Best of Colin Crab and the Ptomaines

The bozos from Editions Zippo have given me 500 words to tell you about Colin Crab and the Ptomaines. Well, I've tried and tried and I just can't do it. Feels like I'm gonna be writing this forever in a weird kind of hell. Who was that geezer—Sisyphus? I know he had something to do with rolling a rock.

When Ron and his crew played their now legendary Empire Tombola gig in the spring of '77, the present writer was, well, present. Not covering the show, but in my new capacity as semi-official manager of the band. From my position in the wings I could see my apprentice, Ali Wilco, notebook in hand, dodging the beer cans as he exchanged muttered words with the Bicycle Records honcho. My girlfriend, Caroline, for once keeping me company as I worked, clutched my hand.

A rock 'n' roll apotheosis seized the band that evening. Bass-player Eugene Winceyette prowled around like some pyjamaed serial killer. Drummer J.D. Drums beat eleven kinds of shit out of his skins. Toothbrush Thomson swung his axe until it started swinging him, and in the process discovered a new and evil variety of feedback. But it was vocalist Crab, smashing at anything electrical that caught his eye, who filled the stage like an octopus, an anemone. When those hydra limbs started whirling, nothing was safe. After a few numbers, the rest of the band started looking nervously at each other, and shrinking to the corners of the stage.

Crab's whooping contralto was wrapping itself round some new material. When Caroline heard the song he'd dedicated to her, I felt her hand go tense, then slip away from mine. For the three minutes it lasted I didn't dare turn round and when I did she had vanished.

But I had no time to worry about Caroline, because Crab was summoning me to join him. 'I wanna introduce a geezer who taught me everything he knows, and he's still a fucking wanker.' Laughter. 'Let's hear it for Jeff Seed!' And before I know what's hit me, I'm shambling on to the stage, dazzled by the lights, deafened by the cheering of the crowd and the boom-screech of the crippled amplifier. 'Hey, Jeff,' Crab shouts, 'Give 'em some of your blues shit.' As if in slow motion I drag the harp out of my pocket and start to play. An agonised wailing fills the hall. Everyone goes silent. This is it. I'm a rock star.

'Let's get the cunt,' Crab shouted, swinging his mike-stand.

It was a defining moment. Sprawled on the stage, while the band took it in turns to hammer at me with fists, boots, guitars, I felt the rage and pain of the street blasting through my nerves like a jolt of electric smack. That was a great review you wrote afterwards, Ali: *tonight I saw the future of rock 'n' roll*. Well, so did I, man. It's just that I don't know how I'm gonna write about it.

The Vegetable Lamb

A hot evening in Xanadu. Even on the edge of the city, where the foothills begin and there are shady pine groves and gardens purple with mallows, there is a heaviness in the air. It feels as if there is going to be a storm soon, but the Consul's wife knows from experience that it can stay like this for weeks without ever breaking. In the mountains, summer storms are common—you can see the lightning sometimes from the garden—but they dissipate before they can get this far. The garden only stays green because the servants water it with water from the picturesque rill, an artificial channel cut by a former Consul from the sacred river half a mile away.

At this time of year, the Consulate in the city is manned by a skeleton staff, and the Consul only drops in for pressing business, returning to his summer cabin to sleep. This is the summer suburb, where all the politicians and businessmen take up residence in the hot season. The cabins have rough, knotty walls through which any draughts can pass, and an overpowering smell of resin, but they're also rather grand, consisting of complexes of separate buildings. The Consul regularly gives dinners for twenty or more on the grill terrace outside the cabin he calls his drawing room. There is a dinner planned for tonight, in fact, and the Consul's wife is checking the preparations at this moment. The long table is laid, the mosquito screens have been checked for damage, the barbecues are beginning to smoke. As for the meat, that is in the kitchen cabin, marinating in olive oil, garlic and herbs. The servants will bring it out at the appropriate time, parading through the dark garden in their white jackets, and taking up their stations at the barbecues. To accompany, a selection of salads and breads; to start, a chilled soup of avocado pears; to follow, the first oranges of the year, with ginger in syrup that has been flown out from London in the diplomatic bag.

She is about forty, slim, with dark hair and eyes that make her look gypsyish, though she actually comes from one of the better families of the South Downs. At present she is wearing a simple blue afternoon dress, but she is planning to change into something slightly more impressive for the dinner. They eat late here, because of the heat, and she has nothing much to do for the next hour or so, as the servants are taking care of all the preparation. It is getting dark in the garden and the fireflies are starting to flicker on the edge of the pines. They always make her think of invisible men waving cigarettes.

She moves round the table, checking the place settings again, though she knows they are all right. Every now and then she goes to the mosquito screen and looks out into the dusk, as if expecting something.

Beyond the foothills of the summer suburb, the mountains begin, grassy and empty. The sheep winter in the valleys between and are driven out in the first fine days of May by bare-legged shepherds to their summer pastures in the uplands. It is a hard life in those high places. The shepherds live in caves, or in rough shelters of stone and moss. At night, even in July and August, the temperature can fall to freezing, while by day the sun is scorching, and there are also thunderstorms, accompanied sometimes by drenching rain, sometimes by hailstones large enough to break bones. Many of the sheep die in these conditions, either from the hail, exposure or falls from the precipices, but enough survive to return in the autumn. Besides, those that die are not wasted, but butchered on the spot and either roasted and eaten immediately or salted and dried for later consumption.

The world of the shepherds is closed to women, who never venture out into the hills, and indeed other Tartarean men know little about it. Most of them can play a bone pipe or a zither and all have a fund of memorised songs, stories and bawdy jokes, which are recited round the fire every year. Since they are away from home so long, the shepherds know how to cook, and the food of the summer pastures is quite different from the domestic fare of town and village, based not only on fresh or preserved mutton, but also on a variety of herbs, roots and aromatics that can only be gathered in the hills. There is a vegetable that resembles a parsnip and another not unlike a cabbage. There are berries, too, never eaten alone, but always as an accompaniment to the meat, for food in those wild parts does not come artificially segregated into courses; one eats while there is still food to be eaten and then one sings or sleeps. The mulberry, staple of rich men's gardens, grows wild and is said to be far superior to suburban varieties; there are orange berries of the bogs something between a cranberry and a cloudberry in fragrance, though too tart for most Western palates; and, sweeter, a high mountain berry like a bilberry, but larger, jet black in colour and rather poisonous-looking. These are smeared on roast lamb as a relish, much as we might eat redcurrant jelly, or, if the meat is mutton, boiled with it to form a sharp sauce.

Then there is the vegetable lamb.

It is the vegetable lamb that has brought her to Tartary. She is not what they would call real diplomat material, despite her good blood. At sixteen she ran away from home with an unsuitable young man, the first of what she refers to as her semi-elopements, and they lived in France for a long autumn, looking for truffles with a rented pig. Since then, she has moved across Europe and beyond, getting into a few scrapes in the War years, collecting lovers and recipes. She has tasted the ortolan, a nocturnal bunting that is brought up in the darkness of a box to make it eat constantly, then, when it has stuffed down enough corn to reach perfect rotundity, drowned in brandy. The roasted birds are eaten under a cloth so none of the fragrance can escape, and bones and all, if a creature that has led such a life can be said to have any. And, in her North African phase, she tasted the heart of the date palm, which is served only at the most important feasts, a monstrous growth between ten and twenty pounds in weight, delicately coloured in many shades of green, orange and white, with a flavour composed of banana, pine and green almond. All this she has written down in a manuscript that will be part memoir, part cookbook, and will make her famous some day. Meanwhile she is a diplomatic wife more or less by accident. When she met Geoffrey she was scrounging off friends in the British colony, cooking for their dinner-parties and working on her book. Geoffrey helped with the matter of her passport and it seemed a good idea to settle down for a bit.

One of her strangest experiences on arriving at the Consulate in Xanadu was to be taken by Dolgiz to the cellar and shown, in a small alcove beyond the racks of port and claret, a pyramid of cans, many of them rusty and missing their labels, gleaming in the light from the bare bulb.

'What are these, Dolgiz?'

'Soup, Madam.'

'What kind of soup?'

He did not know the English word. Dolgiz had been accustomed, in Geoffrey's bachelor days, to a comfortable life of heating up the contents of such tins with, perhaps, a sprinkling of curry powder for variety. He is not really a cook at all, but a sort of orderly and quartermaster, happiest when sharpening knives and arranging the contents of cupboards; an urbanite in a land where women habitually run the kitchen, he is rather terrified of organic matter. Even a caterpillar on a lettuce can cause a personal crisis and she has known him to leave the kitchen and refuse to come back for hours on being asked to deal with a simple dish of tripe.

Over the course of several frustrating bedtime conversations, she gathered that Geoffrey had bought the

94

soup in a job lot from an English company that cleared out of Xanadu in a hurry when the abortive uprising took place a couple of years earlier, and had been serving it at dinners ever since. 'It's perfectly good soup,' he told her. 'Besides, I like celery soup.'

Geoffrey is unable to understand her attitude to food. Like most Scots, he was brought up to be thrifty and, like the upper-class Englishmen with whom he attended school and university, he has been exposed from childhood to culinary atrocities which have dulled his tastes. In the early days of their marriage he lectured her many times about her habit of going to the market alone and haggling over oranges and peppers for the maids to pick up later. 'I suppose you know they call you the Mad *Ingliza*? Well, why do you do it, Selena? It's what we have servants for.'

Useless to explain to him that the market is the focus of all life in Xanadu. Not for him those chilly dawns in the Pyaz, the stallholders all muffled in overcoats, the colour drained from their wares leaving them like sculpted marble simulacra of fruit and vegetables, the gibbets hung with the legs, heads and intestines of animals, the foreign voices gabbling all round. For her, on the other hand, the marketplace, whether in Xanadu or in Marseilles, Syracuse, Paxos or any of the other places she has briefly called home, is where she is most alive. She has been a Mad *Ingliza*, digging her fingers into bins of seeds and husks, asking for news of the latest spices, since she was a girl. She has no intention of changing her habits for a life of celery soup.

The telephone rings in the drawing room, and she goes inside to answer it. 'Geoffrey, where are you?'

'Darling, I'm at the Embassy. May be a bit late. Start without me.'

'How late, Geoffrey?'

'No way of knowing. Sorry. And the Hillmans won't be coming. They've had to leave in a hurry.'

'Geoffrey, what on earth is going on? It's summer. You shouldn't even be working at this time of year.'

'Lot going on today. Too much to explain. Absolutely nothing to worry about, though. Sorry, darling.' He sounds distracted.

She puts down the telephone, making an annoyed humming noise to herself, and presses the electric bell that is supposed to sound in the servants' quarters. There is no response, but then she is never quite sure that it works. Well, it's early yet. They can remove the place-settings for the Hillmans later.

A man is singing at the bottom of the garden. He sounds drunk. It is a song she has heard before, on her morning visits to the Pyaz, mournfully nasal with lots of bent notes. It was sung by a woman then, and she assumed it was something about lost love, and how men always betray women, though her Tartarean was not good enough to make anything of the words. It sounds grossly ironic in a man's voice, as if he is parodying it. What is a drunken man doing down there, anyway? She should get the servants to shoo him away, in fact she will if he's still there when she gets back from dressing for dinner. She knows she is lingering too long here, but a cool breeze has sprung up in the last few minutes and she is beginning to enjoy the darkness, the smell of charcoal, the in-between feeling. Her lover Rodericj is coming tonight, the first time she has dared to invite him.

Rodericj is small and boyish, with Etonian vowels and Tartarean eyes and just the faintest touch of gold in his complexion. She knows less about his background than she should, having met him in the Pyaz over the bins of chillies and asafoetida early one morning, and spent a series of guilty afternoons in his tiny flat full of sacks of potatoes and vats of fermenting apricot wine. He made her laugh by handing her his card in bed, though he was quite serious about it; it described him as an exporter and importer of foodstuffs. He knew without asking about her interest in the vegetable lamb. No, he said, he had never seen one, but he knew a fellow that might be able to get some of the preserved meat. Preserved how, pickled? He thought not, probably dried, in slices, like biltong. You can eat it just as it is, or soak it in boiling water, when it goes soft and fluffy. Quite a good flavour, he'd heard, though different from the fresh. One of the things that keeps her coming back to that flat, covering her face with a scarf as she dodges through a succession of washing-hung courtyards and climbs the rickety fire escape to the top floor, is the promise of that dried vegetable lamb, which he will have waiting for her next time, but which she knows by his smile as he opens the door hasn't turned up yet.

Rodericj finally took her on a long and dangerous afternoon drive to a slumped stone village deep in the foothills to meet his 'fellow', a tough, shrivelled Tartarean called Barometz, who explained, in Rodericj's excited translation, that he was about to start his yearly journey to the interior in search of new specimens. If she ordered a lamb, she could have it when he got back, not exactly fresh, but not exactly dried either. 'They don't go off,' Rodericj said, 'not in the way actual meat does.' And last night he telephoned—fortunately Geoffrey was in town—to say that the lamb had arrived, and he had seen it. 'Darling, it's beautiful. You've never seen anything like it. It's exactly the way Marco Polo described. Must go, see you tomorrow.'

A course on its own, perhaps, the way the French serve *charcuterie*, after the soup? It would be the talk of Xanadu, though she is not particularly interested in having a social triumph. Nor, on the other hand, does she want to keep the lamb to herself—she loves food, but has never been greedy. Besides, she has her doubts about exactly how delectable it really is. Most of the reports date from the Middle Ages, when people had some peculiar tastes: the meat is like fish, apparently, and the blood like honey. It is probably more of a curiosity than anything—it's just that she needs it for her book. It is the last of the delicacies.

The first guests will be here in half an hour and Selena finally rouses herself and goes back to her cabin to dress. In her absence, the darkness seems to increase. Insects are battering thickly at the mosquito screen, trying to get at the electric lights. In the more extreme blackness of the woods, the fireflies are forming and re-forming their low-flying constellations. There are the signs of a storm in the distance, a flickering in the sky and the muffled noise of thunder. The voice at the bottom of the garden continues to sing about the man who has deserted him, left him alone in his little village to drown himself in the fast-flowing river, except that he has been joined by another voice now, and they no longer sound drunk, but more like men who are trying to start a chorus, work up a bit of communal enthusiasm; they sing slowly, with great emphasis, slightly out of phase with each other. The lights are on in the servants' quarters, but the door stays shut and no Dolgiz or Orzic emerges to clear up the place settings for the Hillmans or carry out little dishes of peanuts and olives. There is an odd atmosphere, busy on the edges where it should be still, still in the centre, where it ought to be busy. Then the telephone starts ringing in the drawing room.

She is wearing a festive red that matches her lipstick, and her heels are long enough to be elegant without being quite sharp enough to catch in the gaps between the planks. She has missed three telephone calls already while fastening the dress (on her own, for the maids have gone missing, too) and doing her face. The servants should have been here ages ago. Just as she is preparing to go to their quarters and shout them out the telephone rings again.

The voice on the other end is Tartarean. 'Mrs Crawford,' it says, 'Mrs Crawford.'

'Yes, who is that?'

'Xhrrhxhrrhxhrrhxhrrhxhrrh.'

'I'm sorry, I didn't quite catch that. Could you speak a little louder, please?'

'Xhrrhxhrrhxhrrhxhrrhxhrrh of the Interior. It is about the passports.'

'What about the passports? Whose passports? It's a very bad line.'

'Xhrrhxhrrhxhrrhxhrrhxhrrh bad time.
Xhrrhxhrrhxhrrhxhrrhxhrrh about yxrrh husband.'

'Geoffrey? What about him?'

'Xhrrhxhrrhxhrrhxhrrhxhrrh passpxrrhs.'

'Yes, if you have any enquiries about passports, the place to call is the Consulate. In town. Not here, this is a private residence. I'll give you the number, if you like. It's—'

'Xhrrhxhrrhxhrrhxhrrhxhrrh line. Will ring back.'

'Oh, all right.' She puts the receiver down and waits for a few minutes, but the call does not come. She may have misunderstood the man when she thought he said he was going to call again. Or the line may have given up the ghost altogether. The thought crosses her mind that it could have been someone important and that she was a little short with him. But after all, she is in a hurry. The guests will be arriving any moment. She has no time to answer telephone calls.

She slips out of the porch on to the sinuous path that connects the cabins. It is supposed to be well-lit here, because the servants must walk up it bearing food and drinks, but several of the bulbs have failed. No time to replace them now—Dolgiz must see to it in the morning. The door of the kitchen cabin is ajar, soft light spilling out. She pushes it open.

The cabin is simply furnished, with a woodfired stove in one corner and, in another, a metal-lined larder in which the soup and oranges are resting. Strings of onions, garlic bulbs and peppers hang from the rafters. In the middle of the room is a great pine table laden with shallow, cloth-covered pottery bowls full of oily meat: beef, pork, chicken and the ubiquitous lamb. Lemons are scattered among them, some cut in half, together with bunches of fresh and dried herbs and little piles of chopped parsley. She picks up a kitchen knife, its blade decorated with a smudge of lemon juice and chopped leaves. The scene might be a painting. If only there were some skilful watercolourist present, to capture it for the cover of her book; it would be hard to find a better image for the life she has lived, its sensuousness and earthy confusion. But no illustrator could depict that smell of lemon, herbs, garlic and meat juices with pinewood underlying everything and a hint of smoke creeping in from outside. If she were in England now—well, she would not be expected to go near the kitchen in any case, but it would make no difference, the smells would permeate the entire house, boiled cabbage, boiled tapioca, steamed puddings, all mixing together with the laundry. Why is it that in England everything must be boiled? Perhaps for us cooking and laundry really do belong together; the food must be sanitised before it is brought to the table.

Dolgiz and Orzic are nowhere to be seen. For a moment the thought is quite exciting: she will do the cooking herself, carrying the meat to the barbecue, getting the guests to help, as if they were all peasants together. That is how it ought to be done—there is very little pleasure in food unless you are prepared to get your hands dirty. But no, she is the Consul's wife, and must go and call the servants to order. Lying on their backs in their cabin no doubt, smoking their disgusting cheroots. But as she turns to leave, she finds herself reluctant to step out again into the dark, and even more so to head off further down the path away from her own living quarters. She stands at the door listening for the singers. Nothing. No, wait a moment, there is a sound except that it is not singing any more, but an instrument, thin and hollow-sounding, playing the same sad tune. She recognises it as a bone pipe, having heard a beggar playing one occasionally. It is faint and disappears altogether for a while, so that she wonders if she has heard it at all, but then it returns, stronger and in a different rhythm, choppy and jaunty, though the tune has not changed. Well, she has to go down there to shout out the servants and when she does she will just shout out those singers and the piper as well. Then the telephone rings again in the drawing room and she runs back up the path to answer it.

'Selena.'

'Rodericj, darling, I wish you would hurry up. I'm having quite a peculiar evening. Geoffrey isn't here and the servants have gone missing and the guests will be here any moment —'

'Selena, I'm sorry. I can't come tonight. Very busy. Sorry about it, but—'

'Rodericj, what do you mean? Of course you must come. I've been waiting months to invite you. This is our special evening. And what about the vegetable lamb?'

'Oh, the vegetable lamb?' Rodericj sounds confused, as if he's not quite sure for a moment what she's talking about. And isn't there some whispering going on in the background?

'Rodericj? Have you got anyone with you?'

'Of course not, darling.' Whisper, whisper, whisper.

She is angry suddenly. 'Listen, Rodericj, I don't care if you've got anyone with you or not. I'm too old to play boyfriends and girlfriends. And I'm married anyway, if it comes to that. I just wanted you to be here tonight. I expected it of you. You had a… an official invitation, from the Consul. It was the least you could do.'

'Um, there's nobody here. Selena—'

'What?'

'About the vegetable lamb.' He sounds out of breath, perhaps even panicky. 'I spoke to Barometz, all right? He's bringing it himself. This evening. Because I can't come. You will have it.'

'I don't care about the bloody vegetable lamb, Rodericj. To tell you the truth, I don't believe it exists and I don't care whether it does or not. I just want to know what's going on.'

'You will have it,' Rodericj repeats. And then, echoing her, 'It's the least I can do.' He hangs up without saying goodbye.

She is surprised to find that there are tears in her eyes. She must be getting worse at these moments. She wasn't even aware that she had any feelings for Rodericj except amusement at his enthusiasms. Hardly one of her great loves, anyway. She is just a little stung at having had the brush-off that way, over the telephone at a time when everything else seems to be going wrong. It's the last straw, somehow.

Already, a car is drawing up on the gravel parking area over to the side of the cabin. The first guest. Damn, damn, damn. She hopes it will be someone military. Then she can come over helpless and get him to shout those people out for her. She runs out on to the grill terrace and tries to make out who is in the car. The headlamps are still on, dazzling her, and no one shows any sign of getting out. Perhaps she should go down and welcome whoever it is, in the absence of any servants to do the honours. As she hesitates, the telephone rings again.

'Who is it?'

'Xhrrhxhrrhxhrrhxhrrhxhrrh.'

'Not again, please. I'm sorry, I can't talk. And you obviously mustn't telephone on this line, it just doesn't work.'

'Xhrrhusband. Xhrrhxhrrhxhrrhxhrrhat once.'

'I'm sorry, I can't understand a word you're saying, and I must go.'

She is aware of the noise of a car behind, not arriving, but starting up. She turns round and moves as far as she can towards the window without actually putting the receiver down. The car that arrived a moment ago is leaving again. The sight gives her the bizarre feeling that time is running backwards—not that the car is actually reversing. Meanwhile the voice continues to roar and crackle in her ear.

'What's that? I'm sorry.'

'Xhrrhxhrrhxhrrhxhrrhxhrrhnow. Xhrrhxhrno delay. Xhrrhxhrrhxhrrhxhrrhxhrrhonce. Please. Now.'

The voice is cut off. At the same moment the light goes out. She gropes her way to the grill terrace, only to find that the lights are out there, too, and in the other cabins. The only light comes from the orangey glow of the barbecues. Even the fireflies down in the pinewoods seem to have been extinguished. The singing has returned at the bottom of the garden, this time with many voices, like a male voice choir. In the distance, the storm is still flashing and booming, but isn't it in the wrong direction, over the city rather than the mountains? She watches it, unable to move for a moment, remembering a similar experience in France, and another in Greece. So it's starting again. They seem to be following me about, she thinks, the gunfire and explosions. Perhaps some people are like that; there are people who attract lightning. But that's ridiculous—after all, she is perfectly all right, while Geoffrey and Rodericj are in the thick of it. She must go in at once, and telephone. But still she is unable to move. The singing at the bottom of the garden has been slowly shifting its position, and now it appears to be coming from the servants' quarters. The electric light has not resumed, but there is some illumination down there now, torches probably. There are other sounds, too, scuffling and the occasional thump or crash, as if they are throwing their beds round the cabin.

Finally she returns to the drawing room, locks the door behind her, and makes her way, half crawling, to the telephone. The line is dead. And to think she has been cursing it all evening. Well, she has been in worse spots than this. In Greece she was only a few hours ahead of the

Germans and had to leave everything she had behind. She doesn't even know for certain that anything is happening yet, just noises and lights and absence of lights. But something is happening, and this time there is nowhere to go.

There is a heavy step on the grill terrace, a man's step, and Selena braces herself. 'Madam,' a voice calls.

Naturally, she doesn't answer. They may not know she is there.

'Madam.' Now there is a knock on the door. She does not move.

'Madam. It is Barometz. I bring it.'

A trick. She doesn't reply.

'Madam, I bring lamb, vegetable lamb. Please, open door.'

The vegetable lamb, or lycopodium, is to be found only in the highest and most remote grasslands of Tartary, an area where even the shepherds seldom venture. Sir John Mandeville describes it as a plant bearing large pods, each of which, when split open, contains a perfect miniature lamb. According to other, more reliable, accounts, there is only one lamb, and the plant consists of a rosette of dark green, hairy leaves, out of which, every seven years, a long spiky stalk grows. A single flower forms, white and about the size of a soup-plate. It has an odd, savoury smell which attracts flies in huge numbers for the month or so that it remains in bloom. Then it begins to go woolly, turning into a ball of fluff, which extends from the flower on a sucker, inching towards the ground. When it is nearly touching, the bud starts to develop legs and a head and by the time it has reached, there is a fully formed lamb, still joined to the mother plant by a cord of stalk. It is another week before it is sufficiently developed to move, but then it begins to feed, cropping the grass in a perfect circle around its pivot. It can survive like this for several years, growing bigger and stronger, if it is only allowed to live, but most are eaten by wolves, and a very few are taken by hunters like Barometz, who kill it easily just by cutting the cord. The wool is said to be more precious even than the meat, as fine and warm as vicuña, but as it takes dozens of lycopodiums to make a single coat, few people have ever seen one. The meat, though, is a different matter. If you were to make your way to Tartary, which has been closed to tourists for many years, you might just find a carcass on sale in the Pyaz. If you are exceptionally lucky, it might even be fresh.

The meat is sometimes described as tasting like fish, which only means that, in its dried and reconstituted form at any rate, it is soft and in itself rather bland. But fresh and eaten raw, the fibres oozing with blood, if that dark sticky juice can be called blood, the flavour is extraordinary, more like honey than anything else, but honey that is as fragrant as lavender, as dizzying as burgundy. A curiosity, you might say, but what a curiosity. It is worth seeking out.

Edward's Garden

My uncle Gilbert was the head of the family, a distinction which entitled him to a large and crumbling house in Worcestershire and very little else. My parents and I visited him at intervals during my childhood and I always took away with me an impression of great sadness. I read a good deal as a boy and had a special liking for stories of desert islands —well, Gilbert was cast away on one. If I had to identify him with any character in particular it would have been Ben Gunn, who yearns for toasted cheese. I picture him always at an upstairs window, licking his lips under the enormous grey moustache he affected and longing for toasted cheese. A childish fancy, of course. I imagine you can get toasted cheese as easily in Worcestershire as you can in London. And besides, his life cannot have been as neglected as all that, since he had a staff of sorts, though quite what they did in the house and garden defies the imagination.

We never stayed overnight when we called, and my mother always encouraged me to see it as a philanthropic act, like prison visiting. She said it would make me feel better in the end. We used to visit in summer and picnic in the grounds— I have a perhaps unworthy suspicion that my mother thought it was unsanitary to eat in the house. As a result, the house itself was a sinister place to me. On the occasions when I went inside—sent to fetch my uncle's pipe, say—it was dark and cold after all the sunshine, smelling of strong wood, whisky and damp. There were threadbare oriental rugs rumpled on the floor, chairs piled with forty years' issues of *The Illustrated London News*, dead moths dried and brittle in the corners, scratchy noises behind the skirting.

It was a relief to get back to the garden, neglected as it was. It is impossible to feel really squalid in bright sunshine, as my parents well understood; they picked the days of our visits very carefully. Also, the croquet lawn was easily the most respectable part of the entire estate, since my uncle could see it from the window of the breakfast room, his preferred sanctuary, and the gardener was therefore obliged to keep it trimmed. We used the croquet lawn for picnicking only—I don't think it had been used for croquet for many years, if at all—and I never found the hoops, balls and mallets, though I looked sometimes in the outhouses.

The part of the grounds I liked best was the kitchen garden, which was quite savage. There were still a few vegetables in it, mostly cabbages grown to baobab-like proportions and eaten into fantastic fretwork by the slugs, but I went there for the fruit. At the end of every meal, I was given a basket and allowed to go and fetch as many raspberries, loganberries, red, white and black currants as I could find. The bushes had become ferocious brambles, higher than a man's head, and it was in fact easier for me to penetrate them from underneath like an explorer entering a jungle than it would have been for an adult to pick the fruit at a decorous arm's length. I spent some happy hours under those bushes, collecting fruit, scratches and splinters, sharing the obscure world of greenfly, caterpillars and red mites. Often I did not emerge with my basket until after tea, and then I was not permitted to eat the fruit straight away (I had had my fill from the branches in any case), but had to take it back to London with me. There was the usual embarrassing ritual of goodbye, when my uncle shook my hand and pressed a shilling into it with a wink and a twitch of his moustache, and then we drove back to the station, leaving him with his presumed dreams of toasted cheese.

He must have been missing something, anyway, because one day we received a telegram informing us that he was married. It was the old story, I suppose—at least, I have never really worked out what the old story is, but I dare say it goes something like this. She was in her twenties and a schoolmistress or a secretary. They met when he was on one of his rare trips to town, either in Harrod's or Paddington

Station. There was some little incident: he picked up a dropped parcel or found her a taxi or lent her a handkerchief and love made the usual arrangements. My parents, indecisive as always, could never make up their minds between the unscrupulous treasure-hunter version of the story and the breath-of-spring-in-Gilbert's-musty-life version. If she was a treasure-hunter, she was a naive one, for the mansion she acquired was a simple liability and my uncle had no assets to balance against it. One can imagine her feelings on first inhaling the wood and whisky of the drawing-room.

Whatever version my parents chose, it is a fact that we stopped visiting the house in Worcestershire. In due course, my cousin Edward was born, and my uncle Gilbert, after a decent interval, died in the breakfast room in the middle of the *Times* crossword puzzle. News from Worcestershire was like the bulletins from a remote and uninteresting war in those days. When I heard of Gilbert's death I said to myself, as it were, 'Oh, is that still going on?' Well, it continued to go on, with fewer and fewer bulletins, until Edward went up to Oxford. As an undergraduate he paid a couple of calls on me when in London and I thought him a generally modest young man with a dash of something corrosive in his character, something that might repay further study if I had time. Only when he died and I discovered he had made me an executor—only then did I take interest, and then, of course, it was too late.

The storyteller paused, fiddling with the catch of an attaché case that nestled at his feet. 'I believe you knew Edward at Oriel?' he said.

'Only slightly, sir,' Loosewood replied. 'I'm terribly sorry— I had no idea. What did he die of?'

'Oh well, if you knew Edward even slightly you will be aware that he was sickly from birth. I don't think he died of anything in particular.'

'I really am so terribly sorry.'

'You needn't be. I, too, knew him only slightly. I don't think anyone knew Edward well. I'm bound to say, though, that I know him a great deal better after the last week.'

'You have been sorting through his papers, sir?'

'Exactly.' Everett-Ashley opened his case and took out a sheaf of them. 'As you know, I have a certain reputation in the literary world and I think he wanted me to see his writings and approve them. Yes, I know quite a lot about Edward that I didn't know before.'

My cousin was educated alone, by a private tutor, Williams, a young man just down from university, like yourself, energetic and keen—perhaps too keen. He appears to have loved declensions and conjugations rather more than he loved my cousin, who several times complained of beatings. Edward kept a diary from a very early age, though perhaps *diary* is not the right word. A plural title might be more appropriate, Edward's *cahiers* if you like. It was a logbook of the imagination, complete with maps. Edward used to escape from his persecutor into the garden, which he converted into a personal jungle, just as I had before him, and his papers describe his adventures there in great detail. After an initial phase of amateur naturalism, during which he measured spiders' webs and drew pictures of animal tracks he had found in the shrubbery, one can see him becoming more ambitious. At the age of about twelve, he writes:

> The orchids in the kitchen garden have been particularly abundant this year, including many varieties I have never before seen. One handsome specimen is deep yellow, mottled with scarlet, and attracts a great number of butterflies. The sight of butterflies clinging to orchids in the shadowy light of the raspberry bushes is very fine, and it would need a more

skilful pen than my own to describe it. I have frequently asked both Mama and Mr Williams to come with me to observe the spectacle, but both laugh it off as a childish whimsy. It is hard indeed to be young.

After this entry, the transition is very marked. From the orchids in the kitchen garden, Edward explores further: the tennis court, the rose-garden, the shrubbery and the spinney. And then there are other places that were surely never a part of the garden I remembered—the waterfall, for example, the vineyard, and something he calls the Bird House. There is Bee Valley, about which he writes:

I came out from between two trees and there it was, a sort of green funnel of land between high rocky banks. The steep sides seemed to collect the sunshine and there was a warm, sleepy feeling in the air, although when I left the kitchen garden a cool wind had been blowing. I am calling this region Bee Valley, because I have never seen or heard so many bees. What appeared at first to be a strange, shifting moss proved on closer inspection to be a carpet of tiny alpine flowers, thickly clustered with bees. They form a symbiotic whole: just as the flowers are too close to each other to be separated into discrete plants, so it would be misleading to attempt to separate them from the bees—together they form a bee being. And indeed, the bees are never really separated from the flowers, since they live in the rock underneath, and constantly emerge through small chinks and cracks in it to continue their work on the nectar. I was afraid at first, but found that the bees were too intent on their

food to sting me. This valley is rather bare
compared to the rest of the garden, but I think
I could grow to love it here. Slept two hours,
and returned by way of the Bird House.

There are no people in these fantasies. Like many boys of
his age, Edward seems to have loved animals at the expense
of his own species. As he grows older, the change in his
writing seems to be that the animals become bigger and
fiercer: no longer butterflies, birds and bees, but bears, tigers,
wolves. One particular wolf he tracked through the
shrubbery for many days without ever seeing it. He claims in
his notebook that it was stealing sheep from the croquet
lawn.

'From the croquet lawn?' Loosewood interrupted.

'It's interesting. His perception of the croquet lawn is
exactly the same as mine. He does not see it as part of the
savage world of the garden. Its grass seems still to have been
kept fairly short and this allowed Edward to pretend that it
was cropped by sheep. The croquet lawn, as I mentioned,
was situated outside the breakfast room, which he refused to
enter. It was the room where his father used to do the *Times*
crossword puzzle and where he eventually died. Several
times his mother and Williams tried to force him to enter it
—Williams said that he might otherwise develop an
hysterical personality—but no threats would induce him to
do so.'

'I don't see what this has to do with the garden,'
Loosewood said.

'Heaven knows, I'm no psychologist,' Everett-Ashley
replied, 'but I think there was a dualism in Edward's mind
between the house and the garden. The house represented
his father's death and his own captivity, while the garden was
the place where his imagination could run free. The fact that

a wolf came from the garden to steal sheep from just outside the sacrosanct breakfast room suggests—'

'That the garden was coming closer?'

'If you like.'

At this time Edward acquired a new confidence in his relationship with Williams:

> I have been taunting him because he is a coward and will not come and look for the wolf with me. Today I pretended to confuse *ludus* and *lupus* in my Latin exercises: *I hear the sweet voices of the children at their wolves. Fortune plays an insolent wolf. Wretched shepherd! You have been playing wolves with the village maidens, the flocks not being guarded!* It is amusing—he does not dare punish me because *audavi illos in jentaculo cenaculo*, as he very well knows.

I have heard them in the breakfast room! The Latin would be unrecognisable to Livy and Cicero, but I think we can guess what he claims to have heard. A lonely young widow, a personable and educated man in the prime of his life—I dare say she intended to marry the fellow once she had talked Edward round to the idea. She can hardly have thought he was beneath her station. In the meantime, well… you and I are men of the world, Loosewood.

Edward continues:

> As for the wolf, it is a fine specimen, the pads fully two inches across, and the pieces of hair I have found are grey. I have told Mr Williams that Wednesday would be a good night, seeing the moon will be full, which has nothing to do with superstition but is because it will be easier

to see him. We can take Father's old shotgun. I
know where he used to keep the ammunition.

Williams refused to go. He said it was giving way to
childishness and that it was bad enough that the boy had
been allowed to persist in his obstinacy about the breakfast
room—an obstinacy of which he had taken full advantage,
by the way—without forcing the rest of the family to join in
his games, or wolves. (That 'family' reveals something of his
own attitude, I think.) But Edward's mama was strongly in
favour of the expedition. She was even willing to go herself
if it would please the boy.

I like to think of the three of them on that moonlit
Wednesday night, traipsing through the kitchen garden and
the shrubbery, Williams clinging nervously to the shotgun
while Edward crouched and showed them the tracks of the
wolf's two-inch pads. I see them ambushing it as it raided
the Bird House, Williams firing both barrels point-blank just
below its right ear, the man and boy carrying its enormous
grey corpse home in triumph, Williams skinning it to make a
rug, which they put somewhere Edward would see it, not in
the breakfast room. A rather charming family picture, if
somewhat exotic.

It never happened, of course. Whatever Edward claimed
to have heard in the breakfast room, his hold over his tutor
was not as great as he thought it was.

'So they didn't go?'

'No.' Everett-Ashley finished his brandy and put the papers
back in the attaché case.

'What happens to the notebooks after that?'

'Oh, they become quite routine again. Edward thinks he
has fallen in love with a girl in the village, he writes a lot of
bad poetry, worries about his health—with some
justification as it turned out.'

'But there is no more about the garden?'

113

'No, it was all over after that Wednesday. Tell me about yourself, Loosewood. Your brother tells me you write?'

'After a fashion.'

'So do we all, after a fashion. Yes, that about sums it up. What do you write, stories?'

'I have tried to, sir. Mostly poems, though. Sonnets and so forth.'

'For heaven's sake, boy, forget the sonnet. That sort of thing is quite passé, you know. All form and no function. I should have thought you would realise that. A writer must create a world, solid and perfect in all its particulars, right down to the birds in the trees, to the fleas in their feathers. You can't do that with whatever it is, abba abba—or are they Shakespearean sonnets?'

Loosewood looked troubled, perhaps unsure whether he was being attacked. 'We don't all have your talent, sir,' he said finally.

'Oh, I wasn't thinking of myself. Well, I must be going. A pleasure to meet you, young man.'

'I suppose they were married,' Loosewood said.

'Who?'

'Williams and Edward's mother. After the goings-on in the breakfast room, I mean.'

'It would have been strange if they had been. There was very little left of them on the Thursday morning after the wolf got in through the french window. I assumed you remembered that from the papers. A terrible case. The police never found out what caused those wounds. They thought possibly a wildcat, which seems only slightly less unlikely than a wolf in a breakfast room. And of course both bodies were naked, although this was hushed up at the time. Good luck with the sonnets, or whatever else. Goodbye.'

The Beehive

There are times when Lorna is afraid, mostly at night, when she can't sleep. Then she gets the most bizarre thoughts, like what if it isn't a baby? All women must have worries like that: miscarriages, stillbirths, the baby being born with the wrong number of limbs or mentally handicapped, but surely no one else has the fantasies she does. Not knowing the sex, she doesn't think *he* or *she*; she doesn't even think *it*; she thinks *they*. In the daytime she feels sleepily content or at least resigned, wandering round her tiny flat eating snacks of crispbread with cream cheese and mango chutney or lying in lukewarm baths for hours at a time prodding her stomach to provoke *them* into kicking and making waves and then the word is just a convenient pronoun for a person of indeterminate gender. But at night, when the kicks are sharper and more unexpected, the word sometimes seems to refer to a plural being. In the dark she loses all sense of where the kicking is coming from, where her body begins and ends. Can her womb really be as big as that? Perhaps *they* have got loose in her bloodstream. In the small hours, there's a fine line between foetus and virus.

Malcolm phones every morning, doing his best to be breezy. 'How are we this morning? Are we a happy bunny?'

'Not very well at the moment.'

'So you're not coming in? Look, have you seen a doctor? I've asked around and apparently you're not supposed to have morning sickness at this stage.'

'It isn't morning sickness.'

'You're putting me in a bad position, Lorn. Technically, if you're off work due to the pregnancy, your maternity leave begins from that point.'

'OK, that's what I'll do then.'

'But you only get twenty-six weeks in total, and if you're fit to work… You don't want to waste it.'

'That's my problem.'

She means that the whole thing is her problem. Malcolm has never come out and asked her if he is the father. Probably if she told him he was he would go all honourable on her, make her move in with him, insist on their going to antenatal classes together, maybe even propose. After putting the phone down, she goes to the window and looks out at the building over the road where Malcolm is drinking coffee-machine coffee, going to quality meetings, thinking up new slogans to put on freebie biros and company umbrellas and probably not worrying much about her now that his nine am phone call is out of the way, except perhaps to fill out the maternity leave form on her behalf.

She was fascinated by the headquarters of Beehive Systems long before she went to work there. It looks more like a pagoda than a beehive, wide at the bottom, narrower at the top, with overhanging terraces every few floors. It's the only office block on the northern edge of town, taking up most of the opposite side of the street, with a carpark behind for its hundreds of employees and, beyond that, only the steep wooded hill that marks the beginning of the countryside. Between eight and nine every weekday morning a procession of Volvos and BMWs passes along the street and another of men in suits goes through the double glass doors, the greys, browns and navy-blues lightened by the occasional woman in pink or orange. At night, however late it is, there are always a few squares of yellow light scattered across its black outline.

On her side of the street there are student houses with handwritten lists of the tenants pinned to the doors, ex-shops with nothing in the window and a few that still function: an Asian newsagent, a bookshop specialising in 'the modern heresies', a greengrocer who refuses to sell fruit from right-wing countries. She has been living here since her final year at university, after which she did a bit of waitressing while looking for something more permanent.

The opportunities would have been greater in London, but most of her friends were still here and she would have missed the pubs, the parties, the late-night talks about relationships and politics sitting on the scratchy, straw-coloured remains of carpet in any one of a dozen rented rooms, the dawn walks to the sea—a life that ended when she got the job at Beehive Systems. And now that's ended too. Her job now is to walk round the flat, have her baths and eat crispbread.

She prefers to think there is no father. That would make life so much simpler.

Her first date with Malcolm was at the Blue Lion, a businessmen's pub rather than a student one. There were people she recognised from work at every table. The ceiling was slightly bowed, with black beams twined with what looked like genuine hops. At intervals there were brass warming-pans and iron agricultural implements hanging down low enough for the customers to bang their heads.

'At your age,' Malcolm said, 'your salary should be advancing in leaps and bounds.'

'I don't really care about money.'

'That's fine, I appreciate that. I don't care much about it either for its own sake—it just shows you where you've got to on the ladder. You need to have a map in your head of where you want to be at any given age.'

'Why?'

'Because that way you won't get left out in the cold. Trust me on this one, Lorn, if you're not on the way up in this company you're on the way down.'

There was an awkward silence, which Lorna eventually broke by offering to buy him a drink.

'Oh go on then.'

Waiting at the bar to be served, she looked round the room. A young company, Malcolm called it, and she could see he was right. At least, the people looked young to her now; though it was a kind of young she didn't have much idea of before she joined. Pastel-coloured shirts billowed over broad backs, hair was so groomed nothing could move it, the women wore suits and perfect make-up. Everyone looked so serious, but everyone was laughing.

'Cheers, Lorn,' Malcolm said. 'You're a star. I was just saying, quality is the future.'

She seemed to have skipped a step in this conversation.

'Quality is the big gap in our portfolio. Up to now we've been operating on the better mousetrap principle, and that isn't enough. OK, if you like, introduce these new bells and whistles that are coming out of R and D, but subject to quality. It's infinitely preferable to have a plain vanilla system that's robust than one with loads of tat hanging off it. Where's the quality control? Where's the quality assurance? Personally I think we could make quality the new buzzword. Quality is our Way of Life.'

Lorna looked at her watch under the table. They'd been here two hours already, and the gin and tonic in front of her was her fourth. She wondered when Malcolm was going to get around to it. She had played this one out in her head dozens of times since they started working together: usually it ended with her rejecting him (sometimes this made him violent and once he burst into tears, but mostly he took it like a man), but there were a few variations where she accepted, and in one or two of those she actually enjoyed it. She didn't like to look too carefully at the yes scenarios, because she knew it was the wrong answer: he was at least thirty, he was her boss, he was probably right-wing, she was still sort of involved with Nick. But it was those scenarios that were responsible for the ticklish feeling she was getting in her stomach and joints, which the alcohol was doing nothing to dispel. If he would just get it over with.

'It's horses for courses,' Malcolm was saying. 'Your strength, as I see it, is on the interpersonal front. You could go a long way in this company.' He was very good at eye-contact, probably something you could do a management training course in. The eyes were light blue, and he smiled and nodded slightly as he talked, creating a rapport, encouraging agreement. He was slim with a handsome but slightly too large head, an effect exaggerated by a receding hairline and long, shadowed chin. Now he was saying something about a field trip next week. 'It's like a picnic. Other side of the hill.'

'Sounds great,' she said, touched. It seemed such an old-fashioned thing to ask her to, like something in an American musical.

'Coffee?'

She nodded, and they were halfway out of the pub before she noticed that she had missed a crucial moment. Outside it was still almost light, with that staring blue of a summer evening. She felt the pressure of his hand on her shoulder. 'Look,' she said. 'I think you ought to know I've got a boyfriend. Well, I haven't really, but we still see each other sometimes. It's complicated.'

'I understand.'

Later, in bed in his spacious, tidy flat that had the same lemony smell she recognised from the office, she felt pleased with herself, as if it was an exam she had passed. He lay beside her, his shoulders covered in dark hair but looking, as men always did in these circumstances, soft and vulnerable. She had done that, neutralised him, turned him from a rampant beast into a faintly snoring child, by means of a sort of X-rated lullaby. If it worked on an executive, a man who wore suits, it would work on anyone. She was getting good at this.

A couple of nights later Nick woke her by throwing stones at her window. Since they split up she had only ever spoken to him or seen him in the small hours of the morning, as if he'd become a vampire. She went down and opened the door. 'Nick, do you know what time I've got to be up in the morning?'

'So fucking cold,' he said, hugging himself. It had been raining and his T-shirt was soaked.

'I'll make you a cup of coffee and we can talk for as long as it takes you to drink it, OK?' Another thing that had happened to their relationship since it stopped being one, she kept having to draw up contracts. 'No cheating,' she continued. 'You drink all the coffee before it gets cold.'

He nodded. 'Fucking angel. Love you like fuck.'

'We talk in the kitchen, all right?'

He was long and narrow with a perpetual expression of somehow cool surprise on his face—not as if nothing fazed him but as if everything fazed him the same amount. She used to think he looked like an exclamation mark upside down. He sat at the table and started to roll a joint.

'So,' Lorna said, 'kettle's nearly boiling, time's running out. What do you want to tell me?'

'Just social call. Didn't really want to say anything.'

'It's bloody late for a social call, Nick.'

'You said you'd make coffee. Makes it a social call.'

She was always irritated by the methodical way he made a joint, holding the gummed papers up to the light to check the tightness of the seal, waving them in the air to dry the gum, rolling the roach between the thumb and first two fingers of both hands, packing down tobacco into a tight ridge, bending low over the block of hash as he sliced it with a razor blade. It was the only thing he did carefully. 'You won't have time to smoke that here, you know.'

He made that noise children make when they can't have something, two syllables, rising inflexion. It probably doesn't have a spelling because grownup people don't use it. *Oh-h? Aw-w?*

'In any case, you've had plenty already by the look of you. Where've you been, a party?'

'Walking. By the sea. All over. Last half hour I've been standing in the road, looking at that place you work. I'll never love anybody else, you know.'

'Shut up,' Lorna said, handing him the coffee. 'Beehive. What about it?'

Nick gave his open-mouthed silent laugh. 'You know there's even lights on in there now? Think they're working this late? Or do they leave them on to scare burglars?'

'They're working.' People there worked both more and less than she had expected. There were the late arrivals to ritual cries of 'Afternoon, nice of you to drop in,' the Friday lunchtimes in the pub, when the office was deserted until long after three, the early unexplained departures to ritual cries of 'Another half day?' But then there were the stints that went on late into the night. Lorna had never had to work late yet and one of her anxieties about the job was whether she was spending enough time on it. Did you know when it was your turn to put in the extra hours?

'You know what I think,' Nick says. 'I think they're doing black masses there. I think they're sacrificing cockerels, or whatever. You heard about that?'

'Of course I've heard about it. I practically wrote the book on it.'

Her job was in the marketing department, answering letters from members of the public: schoolchildren doing projects, careers advisers wanting information, technical journalists seeking amplification of a press release. She had a lot of standard letters on file, so most of the time she didn't have to think about it, just put the correct date and the correspondent's name, print off the letter, make an entry in her correspondence log. The most important part was dealing with the queries about the company logo, a stylised hive with bees buzzing round; it had an odd resemblance to a scowling face, with the arch-shaped entrance as the mouth and the other features represented by irregularities in the wicker-like substance it was made of. There were eighteen bees, long-winged blurry specks swirling out of it in an undulating pattern. *The logo was designed by an agency called Emblematix (now no longer in business), when the company was founded. The bee was chosen because of its traditional association with hard work. There is no significance in the number eighteen.* She sent this response to a variety of communications, some printed and business-like, others scrawled in crayon and full of spelling mistakes and obscenities, all of them suggesting the picture represented Beelzebub, the Lord of the Flies and asking about the company's supposed links with Satanism. Some of the correspondents took the trouble to draw in the lines between the bees, producing a fairly convincing 666.

'I didn't expect you to go over to the enemy. You know they sell skimmed milk powder to nursing mothers in the third world.'

'A lot you care about nursing mothers. And anyway they don't.'

'Cut down the fucking rainforest, give all their money to the arms industry.'

'Grow up, Nick. It isn't like that. They don't… we don't really do anything. It's all about ideas.' And she found herself explaining about project management. 'You have a lot of different tasks, and some of them have to be done before you can do some of the others. So if you're making a pot of tea you have to boil the water first. You can show that in a diagram by two boxes with an arrow between them: *boil water* followed by *make tea*. But if you want to make toast as well, you can do that at the same time. And if you want to butter the toast, you can't do that before you've made it, so you have two more boxes with an arrow between them: *make toast* followed by *butter toast*.'

'I love it. They're paying you to learn how to make tea and toast.'

'Well, it has all sorts of applications in industry. For example, if you want to make a car.'

'If you want to make a car, the first thing to do is to put the means of production into the hands of the people.'

'Of course,' Lorna said, 'but I mean after that.' She pushed the sugar at him. 'The thing is, you don't like them because they wear suits and ties and work regular hours, and some of them are married and have kids. But they're just human, Nick, the same as us. You know, they make stupid jokes and they have affairs, and... a lot of them are quite left-wing, actually.'

'Yeah?'

'It's exciting, all these people just thinking, making something out of nothing. The programmers think up the product and we think of ways to sell it. It's like magic.'

'Yeah,' Nick said. 'Saying the Lord's Prayer backwards. Crucifying frogs.'

You don't believe that kind of crap, do you, Nick? That's only for born-again loonies. You're supposed to be a Marxist.'

'Ex-Marxist now,' Nick said, running the tip of his tongue along the joint before lighting up. 'Ex-fucking-everything. You going to have a drag of this, or what?'

Later, they lay on her single bed, tangled, kicking, occasionally changing ends, for what may have been hours. They were certainly making love, or at least they had done, or were going to. There was probably still time to call it off or would have been if it hadn't already happened. At one point Nick went off to raid the fridge and returned with a jar of peanut butter, which he dug out with his index finger and ate without offering her any. She had been just about to come when he went, but when she complained he said she had come at least a dozen times. That was just laughing, she said. And later still, or perhaps in the middle, the room was full of curtained daylight and birdsong so intense it sounded as if the birds were in the room with them with a lot of drills and oboes and xylophones. It was four o'clock in the morning. One day it would be eight o'clock and then she would go to work as usual and this would never have happened.

On the other side of the hill, where the land flattened out, was a little wooded valley, reachable by a B road, which terminated unexpectedly in a car park. The woods were mostly conifers with a few oaks and sweet chestnuts, widely-spaced and pleasantly shady on such a hot day. A dozen tents or small marquees had been put up in a clearing, and the largest of these was the catering tent, where you could get cold chicken, rare roast beef, salad, strawberries, pink champagne and cold beer. All the men were in shorts and T-shirts, all the women in white dresses. There was the sound of a stream not far away, and the shouts, splashes and laughter of people paddling and occasionally throwing each other in. And a loud buzzing of bees, though you couldn't see them, somewhere high up in the trees. 'I didn't know you got bees in forests,' Lorna said. 'You wouldn't think there were enough flowers.'

'There are some.' Malcolm had had his arm round her shoulders all day, emphasising the point that they were in non-office mode. With the can of lager in his other hand, he gestured at a clump of foxgloves, which proved beeless when she looked at it.

'They're probably laid on by the company,' Lorna said. 'Because of the name. As a kind of living logo.'

Malcolm smiled. 'They own all this.' She wasn't sure for a moment who he meant.

He steered her from group to group, picking off the directors of the company one by one. The more senior they were, the more incongruous they looked in shorts, their legs white and gnarled. Here was Tim Penrose the marketing man, Malcolm's boss, here was Jonathan Steyne the Sales Director and Albert Thomas who was in charge of the financial side. Here was Laszlo Nathan himself, the programming genius with frizzy hair and a lighted roll-up between his fingers, but without any of the body odour she'd been warned about, shaking hands without looking at her. And finally, here was Robin Holder, the Chairman, short, stout but boyish-featured. 'The new girl in marketing,' he said. 'Oh yes, I know all about you.' He spoke very fast, blinking all the time. 'How are you getting on with the devil-worshippers?'

'They're not devil-worshippers,' Lorna said. 'They think we are.'

'Makes a lot of trouble for us in the States,' Holder said. 'It's funny here, but over there it's hit the profits hard. And that's our biggest market.'

'Why don't you change the logo?'

He spread his fingers. 'We should, of course. But then they'll only say we're covering it up. The damage is already done. It was Laszlo's fault. Everything we do is Laszlo's fault.'

'Wanker,' Laszlo said.

'You know, this man has to be kept away from the customers because he scares them. And he's been known to burst into the office and grab all the code out of the programmers' hands and take it back to his attic among the rats and pizza cartons.'

'And then I come back a few hours later and I've solved all their problems.'

'I know, I know. That's why I can't fire you. But you're still a fucking nuisance. You two are an item, are you?' he added, changing the direction of his blinks.

'We are,' Malcolm said.

'Congratulations. Congratulations to both of you. That's a very smart young man you've got there, Lorna.'

Lorna was torn between thanking him and attempting some sort of explanation of her situation, which *item* didn't seem to cover, but he was already moving away and she realised it was a show he put on, the swearing and all of it, and now he was going to do it for someone else.

Later, she fell asleep on the edge of the clearing, her head cushioned on a mossy root, a half-full plastic glass of pink champagne balanced on her breastbone. She was woken by the sound of cars driving away. On the edge of her vision people were shaking hands and saying their goodbyes and she knew she ought not to be the last to leave, but she was too comfortable lying where she was. Snippets of conversation reached her, some of them in Malcolm's voice:

'...as far as we can tell, growth is not one of their goals. We don't know what their goals actually are...'

'...was making my CV look a bit naff...'

'...you're heavily on the critical path with respect to this one...'

'...it was just because someone happened to pick up when the guy from Marconi phoned. Otherwise the contract would have gone out of the window...'

'...it's all bloody crisis management...'

'...in charge of longterm strategy, and the joke is we haven't got any longterm strategy...'

'...if Lockheed is serious, then we're going to have to make some changes...'

'...cost the delivery system... cost the payload... are you with me, Malcolm?'

When she came to properly the remaining people in the clearing were stacking branches in the middle. They were genuine bits of tree with twigs, needles and fircones, which made the resulting heap springy and unstable. Malcolm was standing beside her.

'You've got wine on your front,' he said.

'Shit.' She sprang up and wiped at the pink stain with her hand.

'You can change into one of these if you like,' he said, offering her something. Only then did she notice he was wearing a white robe.

'What...?'

'We've been asked to stay on for the fancy dress. It's a great honour. Bit of a laugh, anyway.'

'Oh, I don't think…'

'They have a bonfire and fireworks, and perform a play, just the directors and top management and a few big shots from the most important customers, and then everybody has a couple more beers and a singsong round the fire.'

'Play?'

'We're all in it. That's why you have to put on the costume.'

'I can't. I haven't got anywhere to change.'

'You can use one of the tents. Everybody else changed hours ago, when you were asleep, so no one'll disturb you.'

The tent was warm and smelled of beer, sweat and pine resin. She took off her dress and put on the robe, which was quite similar, though a more classical cut. She decided not to bother with the cardboard mask, but came out again holding it. Malcolm, she noticed, had a mask in his hand, too. The men in the middle of the clearing, also robed, had finished compiling the bonfire and someone now arrived with a flaming torch and set light to it. It went up as if they'd poured petrol on the wood, a single sheet of flame that frizzled the pine needles and tore itself to flying rags at the summit.

Later still, she was lying in the tent when Malcolm came in and cuddled up beside her. The flames were dancing in front of her closed eyelids, with little forms rising up between them, waving their arms and shouting things. She remembered Robin Holder declaiming something in verse that began, 'Fools, do ye not know…' And at one point Laszlo had been standing beside her with his arm round her shoulders helping her to read a page of writing in a foreign language.

'I don't know how to pronounce it.'

'Doesn't matter.'

'What language is it anyway?'

'It's C.'

'What's that?'

'The language that comes after B.'

It didn't matter if you got the play wrong because everyone was very drunk and making all sorts of mistakes and laughing and falling over. And some people were sword-fighting with burning branches and they were all getting so close to the fire that some of them must have been burned but nobody seemed to take any notice. After a while being near the fire was like being high and the masks, with their sharp black noses and wispy feathers hanging off them, took on a life of their own. You forgot there were people attached—you were one weird face among many, floating in the darkness of the wood.

Malcolm was on top of her now and she reached her hand down to help him in. She was ready without him having to do anything; the whole evening had been foreplay. She knew at once that he was nearly ready to come and tried to calm him and make him take his time. 'That's it,' she found herself muttering, 'good boy. You're doing great.' And felt him relax and settle into a rhythm. Most of sex was a matter of *not* getting excited; you had to turn it into a routine, treat it as ordinary, when, as soon as you thought about it, it was the most extraordinary thing in the world. A man putting this prong inside you that didn't even look like part of his body, that wasn't really part of his body most of the time, and you had to pretend it belonged there, turn yourself into the kind of plastic being that was shaped for it and could accommodate it. She always made love with her eyes shut, trying to concentrate on what was happening inside her, but this time a feeling of discomfort made her open them. It was not quite dark in the tent; a little glow left from the fire and the paleness of the summer sky allowed her to see that they were still both in their robes and it was the way these bunched just under her breasts that was hurting her.

'Can you lift up a bit?' she said. 'Malcolm?'

He grunted. She had noticed before that men didn't like talking during intercourse, like that American President who couldn't walk and chew gum at the same time. She worked her hands round under his shoulders, and tried to push him up, and he raised his head, still wearing the mask. It was so unexpected, she gave a little scream, and immediately his body went into the rigor of orgasm.

And latest of all, after he'd left the tent, still without speaking, she lay with her eyes closed, letting memories drift across her mind. She kept visualising herself at work, the open-plan floor with its wood and textile partitions adorned with graphs, calendars and children's crayon drawings, its blond desks, high-tech adjustable chairs and PCs endlessly knitting and reknitting their screensaver patterns, the hissy dribble of the coffee-machine, the warm *ching* the lift made when it arrived. You get used to things so quickly, she thought, almost as if you're genetically programmed to. There was a rule at Beehive, for security purposes, that you should never let a stranger pass in the corridor without challenging them. She should have challenged him, she supposed, but it wasn't easy in that situation. Was it Malcolm? One man was very like another on the inside. She just sort of assumed, like you do. She would probably get used to this too, in the morning, once she had had time to think about it. But there was no denying it was complicated.

Cargo

From above you realise how much blue there is, complex lines of ripple and crinkle interspersed with flickers of white, an incomprehensible writing with the occasional ship for punctuation. And how little land, a dozen inhabited islands and a smattering of rocks spread out in a long arc. It explains everything.

Language, for example: the islands are far enough away from each other to have developed their own dialects, close enough for trade and communication to have evolved. How they talked to each other before the British arrived is another matter, but now that they have English-speakers living among them the *lingua franca* of the islands is Pidgin, or more accurately Pisin. It uses the simplest possible grammar, the smallest possible vocabulary. *Pisin*, for example, is not only the name of the language, but also a type of bird, delicious roasted over a wood fire. It's also any other bird, or birds in general—the plural is the same as the singular. *Pela* is a fellow (most Islanders cannot pronounce the letter F), from which you get *waitpela*, *blakpela*, and *bikpela*, a chief or important man. And *yumipela*, which means we or us. The possessive is achieved by the word *bilong*. Already you know enough Pisin to say the opening of the Lord's Prayer: *Bikpela Papa bilong yumipela*, Our Father. You never know when a prayer might come in useful.

Religion, too. The islands are Christian, but the sect varies from island to island, depending on which missionary was the first to set up shop. Tunuvu, Vanati, Vinutu, Vituva and Anuti are Presbyterian, Nanuvi, Avutu and Tavata Methodist, Tivana, Tatuvi and Taniva Anglican (rather High Church in the case of Taniva), and Santa Maria del Mare, out there on the trade route to somewhere else, is Catholic. Before the missionaries came, the Islanders worshipped their ancestors and whatever gods they could scrape together from sea, sky, rainforest and volcanoes. On feast days they ate breadfruit, yams, coconuts and roast sucking pig stuffed with roast *pisin*, drank *kava*, a mildly intoxicating drink made from chewed plant fibres and danced naked in full view of the gods and ancestors. Now they work in the plantations, eat rice and tinned meat, which they buy with their wages from the island stores, and go to church every Sunday. And the men are allowed only one wife each.

In a six-seater plane crawling above the blue from one island to another, you remember how far you are from everywhere else. After you've lived out here a few years, you begin to forget what home is like. It's just the place where letters come from, and government directives. And all the things you need, like knives and wire and radios and car parts and rice and canned meat and chocolate and gin and cigarettes, delivered in crates at Port Langold, Nanuvi, by passing ships, or dropped off at the various island airstrips, out of the blue either way. If home had disappeared altogether, Haydon thinks, you wouldn't know it, just so long as the other stuff kept coming.

He would rather be going anywhere else in the archipelago, anywhere but Taniva. The Tanivans have a bad reputation with the other islanders: they are said to be sorcerers and thieves. Haydon doesn't believe such tales, but he has never felt comfortable here. Taniva is an unlucky place.

As they come in to land at the Manchester airstrip, the sea disappears from sight, hidden behind hills and fruit plantations, but he continues to feel it somehow, the dizziness of having been reminded how little land there is, how much nothingness it's set in. The Resident Agent is there to meet him; Phillips is probably in his fifties, prematurely aged by sun and alcohol, with deep wrinkles and a conglomeration of malignant-looking freckles and moles. He has an Islander by his side, a man of about thirty in slacks and white shirt, who takes Haydon's case for him.

'This is Bradley,' the Agent says, 'my police-boy. You can trust him. He's a good lad.'

'*Haudu*, Bradley,' Haydon says.

'*Haudu, Mista.*'

They drive to Phillips's bungalow, officially Government House, though it might with equal accuracy be named Police HQ, or Army HQ, come to that—the Agent can call on any number of native auxiliaries and give them whatever title he likes. The sun is over the yardarm, so once Haydon's things are stowed they sit on the verandah drinking gin and lime. Phillips is a bachelor, which is just as well, Haydon thinks as he stares across the hollyhocks and bougainvillea of the garden at Manchester's main street, a dirt track with the Capital stores on the other side and half a dozen other European bungalows clustered together for safety. 'So,' he says, since it seems necessary to break the ice, 'peculiar case.'

'You read the stuff I wired to you?'

'Yes, as far as it went, but there's quite a lot I need to ask you about. And I'd like to interrogate the prisoner first before I take him away.'

'Of course. And Bradley will show you the place where they were cutting down the trees.'

'Is it far?'

'Other side of the island. You can go tomorrow. Bradley will drive you.'

After lunch, Phillips likes to take a siesta, so it's dusk by the time they leave the bungalow. The electric light is already on in the stores and through the open door Haydon can see an old *blakpela* man in a shapeless hat sitting half asleep on a chair surrounded by dozens of wooden crates. Everything comes through here, everything the island needs. 'Had any thefts?' he asks.

'No. There's been a run on the stores, though. Islanders getting rid of all their wages in one go, getting credit, too, till

I put a stop to it. We used up six months' supply of bully beef in three weeks. And we're practically out of knives.'

The prison is at the end of the street, or rather at the point where the street becomes a road because the houses have run out. It is in fact, just another bungalow, no different from the others, complete with a dim verandah where Bradley is sitting reading a book.

'How's the prisoner, Bradley?' Phillips asks, adding, to Haydon, 'He speaks English better than I do.'

'*Nogut, Mista*. I bring him his food but he won't eat it. He say he don't need food.'

'What's the book, Bradley?' Haydon asks.

Bradley holds it up and examines it inside and out as if he hadn't noticed it before. '*The Honeyford Poisonings*,' he reads. 'Is not bad but some of the pages gone.'

'The prisoner had it on him when we arrested him,' Phillips says. 'Wouldn't be parted from it. Kept striding up and down the room waving it at us and pretending to read from it in Pisin. Couldn't really make out what he was saying, though, the way he was gabbling. I'm almost certain he can't read at all. But it's funny how these things take you. At the time I thought I must get it off him, as though it was a weapon of some kind.'

'Is all right, Mista,' Bradley says. 'I give him a Bible now. He ask for it, so I give it.'

The prisoner is reading his Bible when they enter the room. It is an ordinary domestic bedroom and he is not handcuffed or constrained, apart from the lock on the door and the closed external shutters of the windows. He is sitting cross-legged on the bed, the open book on his lap. He is short and slightly built, almost childlike, wearing a simple grey work shirt and trousers. It's difficult to judge his age because of the startling white hair, which makes him look ancient one minute and very young the next.

'*Haudu, Adam*,' Haydon says. '*Man kolim mi Mista Haydon, plispela*.'

Adam's lips are moving slightly as he reads. Isaiah, Haydon notices.

'Adam isn't his real name,' Phillips says. 'We checked the records at the plantation where he used to work. His real name is Melevi.'

Adam looks up suddenly, opens his eyes very wide, or rather it's more as if he retracts all the rest of his face so that the eyes bulge, too much white showing. He thumps his chest. '*Adam Ol.*'

'*Haudu, Adam Ol.*' *Ol* can mean All or Old. Either way the choice of name is significant. The Islanders have never really understood the missionaries when they explain that Jesus is more important than Adam, the oldest ancestor, the ancestor of everyone.

'Ask him about the jacket,' Phillips says. 'Bradley, get it for me, will you?' Bradley slips out of the room and returns a moment later carrying a navy blue jacket with brass buttons. 'He was wearing this when we arrested him.'

Ol has gone back to his reading. He turns the page, holding it an extra moment, the way you do when finishing a sentence. If he really doesn't know how to read, Haydon thinks, he's been watching other people very carefully.

'*Adam,*' Phillips says, '*Melevi, wea yu gotim kot? Dis waitpela kot.*'

'Never mind that,' Haydon says. '*Adam, mi tekim yu kalabus, Nanuvi. Ples nogut, yu stapim dea lontaim. Yu tokim mi nau, mi tokim gavna, mi telim yu sorisori.*' It sounds lame even to him. Ol probably knows as well as he does that he has no power to influence the sentence. Theft, inciting a riot, criminal damage… it will be five years' hard labour at least, whether Ol decides to explain himself or not. At any rate, the words have had no effect; the prisoner continues to read, his lips moving silently. Haydon suddenly realises what he's saying, the Lord's Prayer in Pisin: *Bikpela Papa bilong yumipela yu stap insait heven, holiholi nem hi bilong yu, kindam bilong yu hi kamhir, olting yu wanim man hi mekim wok, ontop graun olsem insait heven…*

'Have a drink?' Phillips produces a bottle of whisky and two cups from his desk. On the other side of the door they can hear Bradley apparently haranguing Adam Ol about something, not behaving properly to the *waitpela*, perhaps. He makes a very conscientious jailer.

'Thanks. I feel bad about this thing. After all, what exactly am I arresting him for?'

'Oh, there's plenty, believe me,' Phillips says. 'He can't be allowed to go on like this. There'd be nobody turning up for work at the plantations, nobody at the mission services, they'd all go back to having a dozen wives each and walking around in their birthday suits.'

'And you're sure he's the man responsible for it all?'

'Every Islander we talked to says the same thing. They were getting their instructions from a little fellow with white hair and a coat with shining buttons. Why aren't you working? Don't need money, the end of the world is coming, Adam Ol told me.'

First of all there were the flowers. If they wanted more cargo, they had to put on their best clothes and sit round a table. And the table had to have a cloth on it, and a vase— well, a bottle actually—with flowers in it. They must have seen *waitpela* doing the same sort of thing. The Islanders were spending all day looking at flowers. So Phillips sent his men in to smash the bottles and throw away the flowers. Which was probably a mistake, because it made them more convinced than ever that they were on the right track. Then there were the books, or if they couldn't get hold of a book, they used letters instead. Every islander you saw had a piece of paper in his hand and walked round pretending to read it. After that there was the business of the aerials. Suddenly all the villages had a kind of flagpole in one of the huts, only without a flag on it. They were used for communicating with the dead. The Islanders would sit round and ask what to do and the ancestors would send a message down the pole. Finally there was the runway.

When we first came here, the Europeans that is, *waitpela*, they thought we were the ancestors. They believed the dead were white. They must have been pretty impressed with us for a while. Looks as if the bloom has rubbed off by now.

The road runs through the darkness of the plantations, as dense and disorientating as a rainforest, perhaps more so since the trees are all spaced the same distance apart. Bradley drives with his eyes fixed on the road, double-declutching neatly when the terrain calls for it. From time to time they hear sounds through the trees—men are at work here and there, harvesting mangoes and bananas or clearing scrub with their machetes. They sing while they work and Haydon catches the strains of *Abide with Me* and *Onward, Christian Soldiers*, the words inaudible. He wonders what language they're singing in, Pisin or Tanivan, and whether the sense is more or less the same as the English.

'Was me that catch him,' Bradley says suddenly.

'What's that?'

'Was me catch Adam Ol. We come to the place where they building *ranawea*, and all the *blakpela* see our light on the road and bugger off. All except Adam Ol, he stand there and look.' Those eyes of his in the headlamps. 'We have twenty-thirty fellow with us, but Mista Phillips say, Bradley, you get him. So I get out of the car a bit scared, because he got *masete* in hand where he been cut down banana tree, and I got no gun, but I got fellow behind me with gun. And I come up to him and say come on, man, and he drop *masete* like that, like I tell him. And then I get hold of him but he like a dead fellow.' In the end it took four of them to get him into the Land Rover. His limbs wouldn't move, and they had to prop him against the seat, drove all the way back with him standing there.

They pull up. To their left is a shapeless patch of cleared land. Some of the stumps have been dug out and the dirt replaced, while others are still lying on the ground. The dirt has been stamped down hard as cement. This was going to be their airstrip, their *ranawea*, where the cargo would be delivered.

'Like being detective,' Bradley says. 'Like in that book.'

'Only a lot easier. There's nothing to investigate really—I know what happened. I just don't understand why.'

'Crazy fellow,' Bradley says.

Haydon offers him a cigarette. 'A whole lot of crazy fellows. Where did you learn to read, Bradley?'

'Thank you, Mista. At Mission. I am orphan boy. Mista Cracken teach me.'

'You got *misis, pikanin*?'

'Yes, Mista. In village.'

'And did they go crazy in your village? Build an aerial, come out here to work on the airstrip?'

'No, Mista. My village we are good Christian. We die, we go to heaven. Mista? Where does it come from really, cargo?'

'It comes from England, Bradley. Or other places, over the sea.'

'I know that. How you get it in England?'

'We make it in factories.'

'I know that, too. Not stupid, I learn that in Mission. But what is factory? How you get one? How make it work?'

Haydon smiles. 'I haven't the faintest idea. We'd better be getting back, Bradley, I've got a plane to catch.'

They come over the sea, the ancestors, *papa hi dai lontaim*, carrying with them a cargo of knives, wire, tobacco, outboard motors. They have been dead so long they no longer remember their old home, don't recognise their descendants. They are strange to you, too, their skin blanched by death, speaking the language people speak out there, in the blue. They bring with them the words of power that make men do things, make new trees grow, make planes and ships come.

You work from *sanap* to *sandan*, digging and hoeing, hacking and gathering, in *planteson*. When night falls you walk the long road to your *villes*, find your way in the dark to *haus bilong yu*, a wooden hut thatched with plaited *lip bilong koko*, where your *misis* spends the day trying to grow a few vegetables in the *bakyad* while keeping an eye on four or five *pikanin*. At the end of the week you go to the *sta* with your wages, buy *tin supam, tin bul hi bip, bak rais, paket ti, paket suga, tin draimik*. Maybe you keep *pik*, maybe you share it with *neba*. When the time comes to *kilim* it, you will need *naip*, which will cost you the best part of six weeks' *wokmani*. Cheaper to make one out of the *tin bul hi bip*, the *tin supam*. You need to save *mani* for *taks*.

Sundays you go to *gothaus*, sing *himsing*, say *prea* to *Bikpela Papa*, the *waitpela* god. He is a family man like you: he has *Pikanin*, as well as *Holigos*, which is a sort of *devel bilong man hi dai*, though the *pris*, Mista Cracken, has never explained this bit very well. The important thing, he says, the Important Thing is that we only have One God, there is Only One God, even though there are Three Aspects to his Nature. So you forget about *Pikanin* and *Holigos*, and say all your *prea* to *Bikpela*. *Bikpela* wants you to speak to him with *ai klos* because he is *so bik man no mas siim*. Once you tried *opinim ai* in *gothaus*, and you still couldn't *siim*. This is not because he *gowea*, because, as Mista Cracken explains he is *olples* at once so *no kan gowea* ever. And now you think of it, wasn't there something *pani* about *gothaus* at that moment, like the indefinable change that comes over the world when you drink *kava* (but you don't drink *kava*), that made *olting*, the *neba* next to you, the *pipol* kneeling in front, the *pris* at the altar, shift and shimmer, as though *Bikpela man no siim* were standing in the way?

Mista Cracken says you must not *tokim prea* for Selfish Things, but you *aksim Bikpela* for *mo pik*, for *mo mani*, for *kago*, *olsem* as you would if you were *tokim prea* to *got bilong ailan* (not that you ever do). If you don't *aksim* for these, who else is going to *aksim* for you? Not Mista Cracken, who has *kago* of his own to *aksim* for. It may be that *Bikpela* has taken offence because you *opinim ai*, but you have *tokim prea lontaim*, and still the *kago* hasn't arrived.

That's when you realise *samting go bagarap*. They were not the ancestors at all, but some kind of impostors from the hereafter, *devel hi luk laik papa*. After all, how do you know how things work out there in the blue? You tried the magic of the books but they weren't the same as the ones the *waitpela* had. You tried the magic of the flowers (you were agonisingly close there for a moment), the magic of the aerials. You started work on the runway, ready for when you needed it. Because the end of the world is coming, *stapim bilong graun*. You won't need money any more, or clothes. *Kindam bilong yu hi kamhir*. The dead will be here soon, planeloads of them, wearing their coats with the shining buttons and this time it won't be their skin that's white, but their hair.

Assassin

Suppose you have to kill someone. It is not as if you have any experience. You have never even cut a lamb's throat or wrung the neck of a chicken, and now, or rather in an hour or two from now, two hours at most, you will be expected to take a man's life. You will be very close to him when you do it, face to face like a lover, and you will see the agony in his eyes as you drive the knife home.

You will need the right weather. Let us say, a cool, breezy morning in spring, the snow already melted on the high passes, the mud still thick on the path, not yet hardened and turned to dust, as it will be in summer. It's early in the year for him to be undertaking such a journey. No doubt he has his reasons and certainly they must be important ones, for he is the kind of man whose reasons are always important. To him, that is, and to others, not, of course, to you. You know almost nothing about him, only that he will come up the path from your left, that he will be on a litter borne by four servants, with donkeys, bodyguards and supplies before and after him, and that you will slip out from behind this rock to kill him. The place has been well chosen for the deed. You will be able to see him coming from a long way off, as the first donkeys cross the ford down below, and begin to toil up the path towards you. At that moment, you will be able to shrink back behind your rock, knowing almost exactly how long you have to wait, to the nearest heartbeat. It is perfectly situated for an ambush, at both a bend and the high point of the climb. The bodyguards in front will have already started down—it will be difficult for them to turn on the narrow path with a sheer drop on one side of them. The ones behind, or most of them, anyway, will be unsighted by the bend. One or two will get to you, but not before you have time to act. And that is all you will need, for the place has not been chosen with your escape in mind.

Well, you have to die some time. So why not go in a whirl of steel, sunlight and blood, knowing that you've changed history, even if you are not exactly sure how? You already know what your last words will be: you will go down shouting *Death to the Fatimids!* though you have no idea what it means. The dagger was selected as the murder weapon precisely so you will not survive. Otherwise you might have been given a crossbow or a phial of poison and the arrangements would have been different.

At least you will not be alone. Beside you, as you wait, is your companion, who seems confident, untroubled by doubts, everything you are not. This, too, is the result of careful planning. Always these missions are carried out by two men, so that each can be a support to the other. If one fails through bad luck or a sudden attack of nerves, the other will be there to carry the thing through, or if it never gets that far, if one tries to desert before the crucial moment, the other will be able to persuade him, one way or another, to carry on. That must be the point of the system, though it has never occurred to you till now what you would do if your companion backed out. It is obvious that he is there to keep an eye on you, to make sure you do your part of the bargain, rather than the other way round. Look at him, as he sits cross-legged on the mud, his eyes half-closed, more-or-less dozing as he usually does when there is nothing active to be done. When he moves into action, it will be with the grace that such people always show in their movements, a cleverness of the body. You can't help thinking that your best policy would be to leave the killing up to him. Only that isn't the plan. You will be the one to deal the fatal blow; if he has any role other than the persuasive one, it is to keep the soldiers away from you, putting his bulk between you and them for just long enough.

Your companion must have a name. We will call him Ali. As a matter of fact, we will call both of you Ali, the big one and the not-so-big one (for it wouldn't do to give the

141

impression that you're puny). Only one name between you, as if to emphasise the fact that individual differences are trivial. You know who you are, anyway, so why should it matter? And it's not as if it's his real name, or yours. Where you come from, people don't have real names.

Where you come from—actually you hardly remember where you really come from. You were not much more than a boy when your father was killed in a mountain ambush similar to this one and you were taken away to the castle on the crag, that looked, from a distance, like a great stony face staring across the valley. The memories of your childhood are less clear to you than the months you spent in a cell carved into the dripping rock, waiting to be ransomed. Most clearly of all, you remember the day they let you out, not because the ransom had finally arrived but because somehow in that cramped darkness you had become a man and men were always useful to them. You remember a light so bright you had to keep your eyes closed and even then you were dazzled; you remember being given a bath that made your limbs feel as if they were floating away, and later so much rice and meat that no matter how much you ate there was always more, until you understood what it must be like to be a sheep or a cow, animals that eat everywhere they go. And there was a drink, too, which you did not touch, because you believed it to be wine.

That day was so much clearer than the ones that came after it. In fact, you are not sure how many there were, though they must have amounted to years rather than months. There was some kind of work you did, sweeping and cleaning, there were people you knew, boys and young men you thought of as your friends. Ali was one of them. Or at least a hefty figure in the background when the rest of you were talking or throwing stones at a discoloured patch in the wall. But you were always aware that these days were an in-between time and that real life would begin later, when something happened that had no name. It didn't do to become too friendly with the other boys or men because one at a time they would disappear and you would know they had gone to do whatever it was or to have whatever it was happen to them. You would never see them again. And yet, by a route no one could explain, a faint shadow of knowledge of the thing was disseminated through the quarters where you all lived. You all knew that it was not sinister at all, that it was the best and most beautiful thing that could ever happen to you. And so, in a way, you longed for it, but in another way you were terrified of it, too, because it might be so beautiful you couldn't stand it.

When it came to be your turn, it was like the day they released you all over again, with the bath and the meat and the rice. And the drink they gave you was wine and this time you drank it. Because there was an old man present whom you felt you could trust and he explained that on this occasion the wine was necessary and not contrary to the law. The law was given to man to prevent intoxication, which was a great evil, but there was not enough wine in the cup to cause intoxication. On the contrary, the wine was a special kind which had a great virtue in it and would make you see, hear and feel more clearly than you had ever done before. And not just the things of the physical world, but spiritual things also. So you drank the wine, which had a strong taste between bitterness and sourness and an overwhelming aroma which rose up your nose to your brain, making you feel slightly dizzy. It soon passes, the old man said, and he was right. And now, he continued, you are ready to be taken to Paradise.

It was dark when you arrived. Everybody has their first taste of Paradise by night, with a full moon shining, warm and yellow. There is a bird there, the nightingale, which has this peculiar property that however loud it sings you can never tell exactly where its voice is coming from. All the time you were there, you kept returning to the trees,

143

searching for it, unwilling to accept it was a bodiless spirit as its invisibility suggested. As everyone knows, Paradise is a walled garden, though it is a very large one and from many parts of it the wall is out of sight. It is not flat, but has hills and valleys and from the hills springs burst out and flow into the valleys, eventually joining together into a small river which leaves the garden by way of a gate in the wall. Some people say that the springs flow with milk and honey and wine, but in fact they are only water, very pure and cold. You came upon one not long after you were admitted to the garden and drank deeply from it, for the wine had left you thirsty. When you rose again, the front of your robe drenched, you reeled for a moment and felt disorientated. There was a sudden unpleasant sensation as if a fist had risen up from the middle of your stomach and struck you on the inside of the head.

That was when time fell to pieces. You were walking down the slope beside the stream, and with every step it was as if you started the journey all over. You stood up, you walked down the hill, you reached the bottom. You stood up, you walked down the hill, you reached the bottom. But was it the same hill, or another? All about you in the short grass were small star-shaped flowers of a colour you could not determine in the moonlight. And there was a strong scent in the air, perhaps produced by these same flowers. You wanted to find out their colour, and whether or not they were responsible for the odour, and so you bent down and picked one. Or rather, as it turned out you did not—you had only intended to pick one, and had mistaken the will for the deed. Or rather, you had picked one, for there it was in your hand, already looking a little wilted, as if you had been holding it for hours. And you raised it to your nose to smell it and found that there was nothing there, though the smell was stronger than ever. You knew then that you had already smelt it, but a long time ago and the scent in your nostrils was only a memory. And now, a moment later, you understood that it had never been a scent at all, but a long strand of music floating in the air—not the song of the nightingale, but human music, played on a harp or zither.

For Paradise is inhabited. At any one time there are a dozen or so young men like yourself, novices or inmates or candidates, and many more of the original denizens of the place, its angels. And there are dwellings among the trees and grassy banks for all these inhabitants, though dwellings is perhaps not the right word, for no one takes up residence in them permanently. The bigger houses are made of wood and can sleep several people, but most of them are mere summerhouses woven of basketwork. It was from one of these that the music came. The light from inside was thrown onto the hillside in streaks and curlicues like unreadable heavenly writing that changed over and over as you approached. And you entered and made the acquaintance of your first angel.

Angels differ from women in many respects. The most obvious of these is that they never speak. They are not without language, for they will respond to commands, if, that is, you are not too dazzled to command them. You may command one to sing, and the noise she will make will be very like human singing, but if those are indeed words that come out of her mouth, they are in no language you have ever heard. You may decide to give one a name, such as Layla or Basma or Jamila, and she will respond when you use it, but she will respond just as readily to any other. This makes you doubt whether she is an identifiable being at all. True, angels take different forms, some tall, some short, some thin, some fat, some with skin like milk and others with skin like honey, but can you be sure you recognise each one as separate, rather than as another seen in a different light or a different mood? Perhaps all angels are the same angel. Perhaps as inhabitants of Paradise and the unmediated handiwork of God, they derive from a time before names were given to creatures to make them distinct from each other.

It is not, however, true, that angels are perpetually virgin. At least, from the little you understand about these matters from whispered discussions with the men or boys you called your friends while you were sweeping the kitchen or throwing stones at the patch in the wall, you are sure they cannot be. That would mean they would bleed and how can an angel bleed? On the contrary, it is you who have your virginity restored to you all over again, every time. Because the acts you performed with the angels, or with the one angel endlessly multiplied in her different guises, on silk pillows in the summerhouses, on grassy banks beside the streams, in the ashy dust in front of a great fire in one of the houses when it was raining outside, were never the same act. You were not doing one deed a thousand times, but a thousand different deeds once.

As long as you were in Paradise, time would never come back together again. It was day or it was night, you were awake or you were asleep (remember those dreams? You never did then, either, but they must have been beautiful, because you woke up crying that you must leave them and return to the humdrum Paradise of the wakeful), you were eating a single grape for hours, or counting every drop of water in a stream, or running one finger down the shoulder blade of an angel and marvelling that it could be so complete and yet lack a wing, but no moment of your life was connected to any other moment. Perhaps that was why you kept searching for the nightingale. With some part of your mind you were missing the connectedness of your former life, unhappy as it had always made you. If only you could connect the song with the bird that produced it. And yet the bird itself was nothing to look at, a small grey-brown creature, of use only as a noisemaker.

That was what the old man told you when he came to visit you in Paradise. You knew now, as you should have known

146

earlier, that he was not just an old man, but *the* Old Man, the one you had whispered of with your friends in the stone-throwing days. He was very humble and very quiet, which was why you had not at first understood that he was the one who had made all this happen. Sometimes you thought he was God, but he told you not to make such a wicked suggestion. Are you trying to tempt me? I am the least of his servants, he said, leaving you wondering what that made you. As before, he brought wine to drink, and told you, when you still hesitated, that it was lawful and would help you to see more clearly. And you asked if that was so, why it did not permit you see the nightingale. And he replied: The reason you never see it is that it is not worth seeing.

And one day he said to you, or perhaps he said it every day —it was impossible to tell the difference: This place is your home now. You will live here forever, enjoying the company of the angels and the music and the mulberries and apricots, an infinite garden of moments, each one different from the rest, as each of these little star-shaped flowers is different if you look at them closely. Yes, forever. There is no death in this garden for where there is no time there is no way to reach it. But there is a small thing I want you to do for me first, before forever begins in earnest. Will you do that for me?

And you struggled to understand him. You did not know what before meant, or forever or how a thing could be small, because every thing was equally big in your mind now. But you wanted to understand him, because he said it so kindly. So when you saw that he was nodding at you, as if to persuade you to follow suit, you nodded too, which seemed to please him. I will return when the time is right, he said. Drink your wine.

Ali, you ask, will it hurt to die? Ali grunts, half asleep. His dagger is stuffed into his belt; yours is in your hand. You haven't been able to put it away all morning, constantly holding it up to the light, looking for nicks in the edge, hairline cracks in the blade. You test it with your thumb, careful not to draw blood. It is very sharp and you find this comforting. If I make the kill with the first blow, you think, then... What? You are still thinking of escape, you cannot help it, even though you know it is impossible. Ali will probably hold out long enough for you to watch the Nizam die and wonder what you are supposed to do next. Should you go to Ali's side and fall there with him? Or go the other way, and try to hack through the ranks of the vanguard as they come back up the hill? Maybe you could throw yourself off the cliff—it would be the most painless way and would save you from any prospect of torture if they took you alive. You squeeze out from behind the rock and take a quick look at the drop on the other side of the path. The valley, far below, is green and soft-looking. Difficult to believe it would do you any injury. It is the air rather than the ground that is so terrible; you fear giving yourself to it, the wind billowing in your robe, the sky all round you, with no friendly earth under your feet. Perhaps your real fear is not that you will fall, but that you won't, that you will fly away and be alone in the sky forever.

It would still hurt less than torture. Less, even, than being stabbed.

What are you doing? Ali says behind you. It seems he was not asleep after all.

Looking at the view.

Is he coming?

You hadn't thought to look, but now you glance in the direction of the ford. No, not yet.

Well don't hang around out there. Somebody might see you.

Such as a passing eagle, you think, but you are not on sarcastic terms with Ali, so you say nothing and return to the shelter of the rock. He is on his feet now and looking, for him, a little nervous. Ali, you say.

What?

Do you believe it?

What?

That we will go back to Paradise? When we...?

He grabs you by the front of your robe and holds your face very close to his. You try not to look at his eyes, which are large and soft, with tears in them. Don't, he says. *Ever.*

You used to see the other candidates in Paradise sometimes. Not to talk to—the only conversations you had were with the Old Man. Otherwise, language was not called for there. You might pass another man seated on the grass by the spring, and think, I knew him once. You might even remember what his name was in a former life, but that was beside the point there. If your eyes met, you would not even smile. How to explain it? The other men were no longer distinct people, but alternative versions of yourself, wearing the same white robe, drifting from one moment to the next, just as you did. You might, for example, go to a summerhouse to eat and there was another man, another you, sitting on the cushions, tearing at bread and figs. It would not occur to you to join him there, and eat with him. You would not need to because it would be as if you were already eating. And if instead you found him listening to music or intertwined with an angel, it would be you listening, you intertwined. You would not dream of being jealous or embarrassed. You would only shut the door and go out again. So it is difficult now for you to remember who was there in Paradise with you. But you have two memories of Ali.

Once, you saw him across a fire in one of the houses at night, his great round face, laughing and laughing. Why should he laugh? You never laughed the whole time you were there—there was nothing to laugh at, no language and therefore no jokes. But there he was, breathing in great agonised convulsions, his face red, tears sparkling in the firelight.

And once he found you sitting in the branches of a tree, tearing off the leaves and scattering them all round you. Your robe was torn and the skin of your arms and legs scratched from the branches. He came up to the tree and looked up at you in wonder with his big face. I just want to find that damned bird, you told him.

It has begun to rain now, a fine, cold, mountain rain, swirling across the pass in twisted skeins. The rock in front of you and the overhanging cliff behind offer some shelter, but the rain finds its way in eventually, handfuls of it sliding into the gaps between your robe and skin, while all around you are the magnified noises of drops hitting the rock and turning to rivulets. You put your head out from the rock into the downpour and discover that the view of the valley and the mountains on the other side of it has turned to grey-white cloud.

If he comes now, you tell Ali, we won't be able to see him crossing the ford, or hear him either. They'll be on top of us before we know anything about it.

We'll kill him anyway, Ali says.

Surely he will not arrive when it's raining? It has always been dry and clear when you rehearsed the scene in your mind. You try to go over it again with a blur of rain obscuring it, clothes drenched, hands and feet slipping, blood washing away, the burning pain of a wound mixing with the chill. Whatever happens, you don't want it to be messy, with the knives missing their target, and the killing and the dying parts all confused with each other. If you have to die, you want to die neatly, the way it's been arranged.

It used to rain in Paradise, too. How could it not? A garden needs rain to make it grow and this garden is situated in the highest and most inaccessible part of the mountains, where the weather is never to be relied on, even in summer. To a man who has tasted the wine of the place, rain is not an ugly thing. You can listen to it, bathe in it, meditate endlessly on the way it transforms itself from vertical manyness to horizontal oneness. And in any case there is shelter from it, if the cold and damp have become too much, in the wooden houses beside the great fires. The angels would never allow you to catch cold.

At least, not if they could help it. But only God is omnipotent, and the angels could not reach you once you had made up your mind that you would not be reached and that you would not seek shelter when it rained or food when you were hungry or angelic company when you were tired of being alone. It began with your search for the nightingale, that made you forget everything else, put off all other pleasures till you had found it. You climbed trees, shredded leaves, clambered uncomfortably into bushes, causing no real harm. But as you still failed to find it, a forgotten feeling began to grow in your mind, an unpleasant sensation, but one you had somehow missed. You didn't even know what it was called: frustration, irritation, anger, a barrier between you and your desires. You would just stay out here a little longer, even though it was raining and your robe was drenched and your turban beginning to come unwound.

You were deep in a thicket when the angels started to call you by name, Ali, Ali. Two angels walked in front of you, only a yard away, and did not see you through the foliage. One stopped to pull a thorny twig from her bare foot and made a hissy sound and then they walked on, calling. Something about the scene reminded you of your childhood, of being a boy in the place of women, when they would call for you and tell you what to do. You said to yourself, I will not come out, they will not find me. And as you said it, you remembered that that was what you had said then, too.

Ali is standing out in the rain, trying to catch a glimpse of the ford, while you cower behind him between rock and cliff, looking at his broad, drenched back. The dagger is in your hand. You could kill him now, if you wanted. It would be no harder than striking at the Nizam, far easier, in fact, for there are no bodyguards and the blow would come from behind. There is a point just below the left shoulder blade where the wet fabric clings to a little hollow that almost seems designed to take a knife. You weigh the dagger in your hand and think, for the hundredth time, how light it feels. That is because it is so well-balanced—there is extra weight in the handle—and also because the blade is so sharp. At the edges, it is hardly there at all. A determined shove and you could push it in right up to the hilt, before he even knew you were doing it. It would be merciful to him, too, for it would save him from any chance of torture.

You know this, but it is hard to make yourself believe it. Especially with the rain and cloud still covering everything like a curtain. It seems to you that the Nizam will never arrive, that there will be no murder, no struggle with the bodyguards in the mud, no flinging yourself into emptiness or letting yourself be overpowered and carried off to the torturer. Whatever is approaching behind that veil is so vague and hypothetical that to stab him in the back to prevent it would be an obscenity.

You will just see if you can move closer to Ali without him hearing you. Maybe when you are close enough, you will know whether or not you can do it. If he hears nothing, you will know it is possible; otherwise, you can put the idea out of your mind for good. You rest your weight on the balls of your feet and lean slightly forward to take your back away from the cliff face. A trickle of water and loose stones is released, but Ali has heard nothing. You take a slow, exaggerated step. He doesn't move. And another. Still nothing. One more, and you reach the edge of the shelter, so that you are fully exposed to the rain. Bring the dagger-hand forward. You could touch him easily with the point now, even plunge it through the robe and into his skin. But you are not close enough to do any real damage. To strike a fatal blow you would have to take another step, maybe a run or a jump to get some momentum behind it. You will stop here and think about it. Still no sign that he has heard you.

You are no longer sure where the spot is on his back that you intended to aim for. Perhaps he did move after all when you were creeping up on him. The contours of his body have changed and the robe is hanging differently. The wind must have shifted it. What made you think there was a hollow there in the first place? Backs are hard and bony, and you aren't sure you are strong enough to drive the knife through solid bone into the soft organs beneath. Even if you are, the delicate blade might break under the impact.

And if you succeed? You imagine his scream of pain and anger, that powerful body writhing on the path, the reproach in his eyes as he realises that you have betrayed him. Not that he is your friend. You have hardly exchanged a word for the whole of the mission, except to discuss which path to take and where to stop for the night. But he was with you in Paradise. That makes a bond between you, even though his experience of it was different from your own, even though you fell and he didn't. You can't stab a man in the back when you have been in Paradise together.

I think the rain is stopping, Ali murmurs.

You have been hungry in Paradise. You have been soaked to the skin there, shivering in a little hollow in the ground covered with dripping bushes, sure that you would die of cold before the night was out, or if not, then of fever the next day. You have sat terrified when the angels shouted your name and afterwards when the soldiers came with their swords and bows and shouted curses. You have cursed yourself, too, saying I had everything and I abandoned it for no reason at all. You have seen the leaves grey and sodden,

153

the grass pocked and muddy where the soldiers have trampled it, you have seen the angels transformed to women, huddling together under a tree and talking in worried voices, no doubt afraid they would be punished for having let you get away. You have wished you could undo everything you've done, that you could just get up and walk back to them, saying where is the Old Man, give me a cup of wine, let time fall to pieces again. But you have known that this was impossible, that however much pleasure you could still take from the wine and the shattering of time into moments, it would only be pleasure from now on and that would not be the same. You are the only man ever to be cast out of Paradise without leaving it.

They found you in the end, under the bushes. You were still half asleep when the soldiers dragged you out through the gates and brought you to the Old Man in the chamber where once you had eaten so much rice and meat you reminded yourself of a cow. He was deep in thought, but when he looked up, he seemed almost amused. Well, well, Ali, he said. What am I to do with you?

You knew then that if you said the wrong thing you would die. And that was when you surpassed yourself. You grovelled on the tiled floor saying, Master, Master, forgive me, let me go back to Paradise. Perhaps you even wept.

And he said, Is that what you really want, Ali?

Yes, Master. Please, just let me go back.

But what happened to you? Where did you go?

Master, I got lost. I did not know where I was. And then I must have become ill because everything was strange.

Why did you hide?

I don't know, Master. I was afraid.

What did you mean by strange?

I was in Paradise, but not in it. I think...

What, Ali?

I think I must have been in Hell.

That was your moment of inspiration. You showed him that you understood the scheme of things, that his pleasure was Paradise and his displeasure Hell, and in so doing you saved your life. And brought yourself to this mountain path, to do the small thing he wanted. Ali, you say.

Ssh. He scurries back behind the rock. They're coming.

You slip into the open, for just long enough to see the little figures crossing the ford. There are dozens of them. Ali hisses behind you, and you go back again. How long will they take to get here?

You see that lighter patch in the cloud over there? That's the sun. By the time it burns through, they'll be here.

You look at the sky. There's a fuzzy area in the cloud, slightly paler than the rest, though you wouldn't have recognised it as the sun. Ali?

What?

It was the wine. Something they put in the wine.

Shut up, I don't want to hear it.

You know what they call us? *Hashishins*. It means...

You shut up, or I kill you.

You turn to him and notice he has his eyes closed, his dagger drawn. You lean out for another look and this time it seems to you that you can make out the forms of donkeys, even a long shape that may be the Nizam on his litter. It's a crazy idea to use a litter to go uphill—he must be constantly struggling not to fall off. But that's what it takes to be one of these people, Nizams and Caliphs and Viziers; they have to have luxury even if it's uncomfortable. You look up again. The patch is still shapeless, but a little brighter already. Soon it will begin to concentrate its forces, assume the shape of a circle, burn its way through the veil. You have until then to explain all this to Ali, talk him out of it.

Suppose you manage it. Suppose you stay behind your rock and watch the procession go by, the bodyguards who would have plunged their daggers into you kicking the mud from their boots, the Nizam on his litter lurching from uphill to

155

downhill, then make your own way back in the other direction. There's a little town you would come to where you could put up for a while, spend the last of your money while you decided what to do next. You would have to change your names again, in case the Old Man sent another pair of his *hashishins* after you. You could become farmers, marry a couple of local girls, pretend you had always lived there.

But after all there is no supposing about it. You know who you are. You know what you have to do.

Matthew Francis's most recent publication, *Mandeville* (Faber, 2008), a collection of poems inspired by the medieval travel-writer Sir John Mandeville, received outstanding reviews in *The Observer* and *The Guardian* and his previous collection, *Whereabouts* was also highly reviewed, whilst *Dragons* (Faber, 2001) was shortlisted for the Forward Prize and The Welsh Book of the Year Award and *Blizzard* (Faber, 1996) was shortlisted for the Forward Prize and winner of the Southern Arts Prize. He is also the author of a novel *WHOM* (Bloomsbury, 1989), and of a critical study of W. S. Graham, *Where the People Are* (Salt, 2004) as well as editor of Graham's *New Collected Poems* (Faber, 2004). He is currently working on a novel set in Wales and London in the seventeenth century, and a new collection of poems.